Fawcett Gold Medal Books
by John D. MacDonald

All These Condemned
April Evil
Area of Suspicion
Barrier Island
The Beach Girls
Border Town Girl
The Brass Cupcake
A Bullet for Cinderella
Cancel All Our Vows
Clemmie
Condominium
Contrary Pleasure
The Crossroads
Cry Hard, Cry Fast
The Damned
Dead Low Tide
Deadly Welcome
Death Trap
The Deceivers
The Drowner
The Empty Trap
The End of the Night
End of the Tiger and Other
    Stories
The Executioners
A Flash of Green
The Girl, the Gold Watch and
    Everything
The Good Old Stuff
Judge Me Not
A Key to the Suite
The Last One Left
A Man of Affairs
Murder for the Bride
Murder in the Wind
The Neon Jungle
Nothing Can Go Wrong

One Monday We Killed
    Them All
One More Sunday
On the Run
The Only Girl in the Game
Please Write For Details
The Price of Murder
Seven
Slam the Big Door
Soft Touch
Where is Janice Gantry?
You Live Once

TRAVIS McGEE SERIES
Bright Orange for the Shroud
Cinnamon Skin
Darker Than Amber
A Deadly Shade of Gold
The Deep Blue Good-By
The Dreadful Lemon Sky
Dress Her in Indigo
The Empty Copper Sea
Free Fall in Crimson
The Girl in the Plain Brown
    Wrapper
The Green Ripper
The Lonely Silver Rain
The Long Lavender Look
Nightmare in Pink
Official Travis McGee
    Quizbook
One Fearful Yellow Eye
Pale Gray for Guilt
A Purple Place for Dying
The Quick Red Fox
The Scarlet Ruse
A Tan and Sandy Silence
The Turquoise Lament

JOHN D. MacDONALD

Border Town Girl

two novellas

FAWCETT GOLD MEDAL   •   NEW YORK

Border Town Girl

1

THE TALL GIRL WAS RESTLESS. SHE HAD DARK eyes with a hard flickering light in them, like black opals. Her mouth was wide and soft and sullen.

It was ten o'clock at night in Baker, Texas. Her third-floor room in the Sage House had the hot breathlessness of the bakery she had once worked in—back when she was fourteen and had looked eighteen.

Five days in this hole. And it could be five more.

A half-block away a barn dance was in progress. She could hear the tinny whine of the music, the resounding stomping of boots. Somebody yelled shrilly, "Eeee-yah-hooo!"

"Damn silly cowhands," she muttered. She lay diagonally across the bed. She had thrown the light cotton dress on a chair, the slip on top of it. The heat covered her body with a mist of perspiration. The spread under her was damp, so were the bra and the panties she was wearing.

She threw the movie magazine off the bed, sat up and tapped a cigarette on a long thumbnail the color of blood. As she lighted it a heavy strand of hair swung forward. The hair was the color of wheat, so expensively and expertly dyed that it looked natural. She tossed it back into place with a quick movement of her head.

As she sucked smoke into her lungs she looked around the room. Brown and green grass rug. Wicker furniture. Metal bed painted a liverish green. The mattress sagged toward the middle from all directions. Her two suitcases

8

were on stands by the far wall, the lids open. A stocking dangled out of one, almost to the floor.

"You're letting it get you, kid," she said softly.

In her bare feet she paddled over to the larger suitcase and took the last pint out from under the rumpled clothes. She broke her fingernail on the plastic covering and cursed bitterly. She tossed the covering into the tin wastebasket by the bureau, then poured three inches of the rye into the heavy tumbler that stood on the bureau beside the Gideon Bible.

She stood in front of the bureau, staring down into the glass, hating the loneliness, the fear, the tension. The heavy rope of hair swung forward again. She stood in an ugly way, feet spread, shoulders slumped, stomach thrust forward.

"How, kid," she whispered. She tossed off the tepid liquor, gagged slightly on it, poured some more in the glass and left it on the bureau top.

She went into the bathroom. The big old tub stood on feet cast to resemble claws. She put the plug in and started the water running. The pipes were so clogged that the water came out in a thin stream. She went back and got her glass and went to the front window. Starlight glinted off the Rio Grande. Across the way she could see the lights of small, dirty, turbulent Piedras Chicas.

A faint night breeze swayed the dusty curtains and cooled her body. She looked hard at the distant lights as though trying to see down into the streets, to see the man who would bring the package across the river.

When the tub was deep with lukewarm water she finished the second drink, went in and dropped her damp underthings on the floor. She got in and lay out as flat as she could. She looked down with satisfaction at the long clean lines of her body. She adjusted the angle of her head against the back of the tub. The heavy hair hung down into the water. She yawned and closed her eyes.

A flabby, moon-faced, middle-aged man came quietly down the hall. He wore a sports shirt loudly decorated with rodeo scenes. He listened outside her door, then slipped a paper-thin strip of tool steel out of his trouser pocket. His small pink mouth pursed in concentration as he slid the strip along the jamb. When it touched the latch he pressed hard, pulling slightly toward himself. There was a thin grating sound. He turned the knob slowly and pulled the door open a crack. He looked in, then looked up and down the hall.

He stepped lightly into the room and shut the door silently behind him. He drifted, soundless as smoke, across the room to the half-open bathroom door.

For a long time he studied her, his expression that of someone who intends to perform a difficult act with practiced confidence. Then he slipped his shirt off and threw it behind him. Rubbery muscles moved underneath the flaccid white skin. In two quick steps he reached her. She heaved up as his stubby white thumbs dug into the pressure points at the base of her throat. Her eyes rolled back into her head so that only two narrow slits of white showed.

He yanked out the plug and the water began to swirl down the drain.

Shaymen watched her for a moment and then began an expert search of the room. He slit the linings of the two suitcases, wrenched the high heels from five pairs of shoes, looked under the rugs, in the backs of the two pictures. He found it in a leg of the metal bed. The caster had been pulled out of the leg and what he wanted had been shoved up inside the hollow metal, then the caster had been replaced.

He slipped off the rubber band and the oilcloth. The tightly rolled bills expanded. Shaymen riffled the corners with his thumb. Hundreds, five hundreds and thousands. He frowned. He didn't like the thousands. They called for a fencing operation and a discount. The recent activities of the Bureau of Internal Revenue had made the discount a big one.

He tucked the roll into his pocket and put his shirt back on, looking in at the girl as he buttoned it. Regret stabbed him briefly and was gone. He left the room after making certain that the hallway was empty. On his way down the stairs he nibbled the thin coating of glass cement from his finger tips. It had an acid taste. He spat out the hard flakes with small soft explosive sounds. It was always better than gloves. Didn't arouse suspicion. Didn't smother the cleverness of the hands.

In the lobby he bought a pack of cigarettes from the girl who was just cleaning the counter for the night. He smiled inside himself as he saw her staring at the shirt. It was so flamboyant that no one looked beyond it to his face.

Out on the sidewalk, which still gave off the remembered heat of the sun, he took a deep drag on his cigarette and walked west. The tourist court was a quarter mile beyond the city limits. Travelers sat out in the lawn chairs escaping the heat. They talked and laughed softly. Shaymen accepted the invitation to sit with them and have a cold beer. He was sleepy. He yawned a great deal.

2

LANE SANSON SUPPORTED HIMSELF PRECARIously against the bar in one of the cheaper cantinas of Piedras Chicas. A wandering *mariachi* with a guitar was singing "Maria Bonita" in a hard nasal voice. His income depended on his nuisance value. A peso would keep that nerve-twanging voice at a safe distance.

Lane Sanson cupped his big hand around the small glass of mescal on the bar in front of him. The solution of all eternal mysteries was on the tip of his mind, ready to be jolted off with this drink—or the next, or the next.

An absent smile touched his big hard-lipped mouth and

he thought, You better start finding some answers quick, Sanson. A lot of good answers.

That was the trouble with the world. No answers. All questions. How did Sandy put it that night she left for good? "Lane, you've spent six years feeling sorry for yourself. Frankly, you've turned into a bore." Her bright eyes had crackled with angry flame.

"So?" he had said, as insolently as he could manage.

"Good-by, Lane." Just like that. Clunk. Gone.

Oh, that Lane Sanson, he's going places. Yessiree. That's what they had said. A hell of a good reporter, that Sanson. Did you read his book? *Battalion Front,* it was called. Remember the reviews? "This one has guts." "A war book with integrity." The magazine serial rights brought in forty thousand and the book club edition added fifty to that and the movies had donated a neat sixty-two five.

If his agents hadn't been on the ball, taxes would have creamed him. But the movie deal spread the take over five years and the book and magazine take were prorated backward over the previous three tax years.

One day you're a member of the working press. A day later you're a cocktail party lion.

And Lane Sanson, the man of the hour, spent the next five years breaking Sandy's heart. This was the last year of income from the book. Where did it go, that integrity they yakked about? Diluted over a thousand bar tops, spread in sweet-talk to half a hundred wenches.

And sooner or later you hit bottom. The inevitable bottom. Three weeks ago he had gotten the papers in Mexico City. He had signed them. Good-by, Sandy. There was a party that night. What a party! It lasted four days.

When the hangover was gone he had written the letters. Ten of them. Eight had answered and of the eight, seven had said, "So sorry, pal." The eighth had said, "Come on up for a try. Leg man. Guild rates."

And so he had driven out of Mexico City in the Buick convertible that was beginning to be a shambling relic of the big money year. Six hundred miles of Mexican sun with the top down had put a false look of health on top of the pale dissipation green of the two years in Mexico City—two years with nothing to show for them but fifty pages of manuscript so foul that on that last cool night he'd used it to get the fire burning in the apartment out Chapultepec way.

Yes, he had driven right up to the border, full of false courage, and when he had seen the bridge across the Rio Grande, the bottom had fallen out. On this side of the bridge a man could drift along. Over on that side he had to produce. And Lane Sanson was grievously afraid that, at thirty-four, his producing days were over for keeps.

One stinking bridge to cross, and he couldn't make it. He'd parked the car, wolfed enchiladas for a base, and embarked on a mescal project.

So far he had arrived at one great truth. Up to the age of twenty-eight everything he had done had turned out right. And then the gods had switched the dice. How long can a man go on alienating his friends. forgetting his skills, fouling up his marriage? The loss of Sandy was a pain that rattled around in his heart. Sandy of the gamin smile, the quick young body, the eyes that could go solemn on you. Sunday mornings with Sandy. Sandy whom he had struck, hearing her emit a low soft note of pain that stung his drunken heart because it was the same soft sound she made when ecstasy was too much to bear silently.

He doubled his fist and struck the edge of the bar. Damn a man who rolls endlessly down a bottomless slope and cannot save himself.

An Indio girl moved close beside him. She had a flat broad brown face, obsidian black expressionless eyes and a wide mechanical inviting smile.

"*Por favor,* buy Felicia a dreenk, señor," she wheedled.

She wore a cheap cotton dress, pale blue plaid, that was too small for her. It stopped short above her bare brown knees and was pulled to a dangerous tightness across her high bold breasts. With the lights behind her, it was very obvious that she wore nothing but the dress. Her feet were bare and broad.

"Your ancestors were kings," he said, slurring his words. "They had a great civilization."

"Just wan leetle dreenk for Felicia?"

"They sacrificed young virgins to the sun god, Felicia. At dawn from the top of mighty pyramids."

"Here the tequila ees good. I like."

He pushed two pesos across the bar top. The bartender filled a small glass for Felicia. *"Muchas gracias,"* she said.

"Salud," said Sanson. He touched her glass with his glass of smoky mescal and they drank.

"Wan more now?" Felicia said.

"No more now, darling."

There was a thin flare of contempt far back in the depths of the shining eyes. "You buy Felicia more, Felicia make you happy."

"That is the terrible goal of mankind. To be happy. I wonder if it is a good thing, this pursuit of happiness. What do you think, Felicia?"

"No understand."

He noticed that her shining black hair had been frizzed into a cheap permanent. "Happiness?" he said. "I no understand either."

"Wat your name? How called you?"

"Lane," he said. She repeated it twice.

He bought her another tequila. It disappeared like magic. Her eyes had a brighter glow.

"I luff Lane. Lane luff Felicia. Good?"

"That, my dear, is the ultimate simplification."

"No big words. Too much big word. No unnerstand. We go now?"

"Where do we go?"

"Lane come with me to be happy. To a place."

He looked at her, at the hip-shot stance, at hard heavy breasts bulging blue plaid cotton, and was tempted. He remembered a drunken party in Acapulco, how on the way back he and the Mexican colonel had stopped off in Tierra-colorado, remembered the stench of the hut, the small children sent out to giggle in the darkness while he and the colonel slept with the women.

"It would be too much happiness," he said.

"Maybe," she said dubiously, "other cantina first? How you say, *más barato*."

"Cheaper."

"Ah, si! Cheepair!"

He shoved the change from the bar top into his pocket. It no longer mattered what he did or said, where he went or why. He staggered heavily when he got away from the support of the bar. She grabbed him with a strength quite astonishing and steadied him. A group of Mexicans stared at him and chortled. Sanson was perfectly aware that disaster lay ahead. With luck all they would do was roll him for what cash he had. And somehow it didn't matter.

The cantina lights revolved sickeningly and he struck the side of his face against the door jamb. She pulled him erect and steered him out into the furnacelike air of the night. She held his arm clasped tightly against her and he felt the sleek play of her muscles under the taut brown skin as she struggled with him, trying to steer him down the sidewalk.

"No far. No long way," she panted.

They came to the dark mouth of a narrow fetid alley, full of the stink of decay. She looked behind them and then shoved him into the alley, shoved him with such explosive strength that he stumbled and fell heavily on elbow and hip. He felt his lips twist upward, half in pain and half in grim humor. It was coming a lot sooner than he expected. If his luck held out, they would slit his throat. And that was something he had thought of doing himself, standing, looking into his own bathroom mirror.

He was yanked to his feet and slammed against the building, hard. He saw Felicia out on the sidewalk, looking in the other direction. He could make out the wavering figures of two men who stood close in front of him.

"Where is it?" a man demanded in whispering, metallic English.

"Hip pocket," Lane said.

"Hands high."

He obeyed. His wallet was taken out of his hip pocket.

A pencil flashlight flicked on, pointed at the sheaf of bills. Suddenly the wallet was slapped hard against his mouth. He felt the blood run between his teeth.

"This is just money. Where is the package?"

"I don't know what you're talking about," Sanson said with drunken dignity.

"You are the one. We know you are the one. No one else has come. Don't try to play games."

"You've got the wrong guy," Sanson said querulously.

There was a sudden pin-prick against his belly. The light flicked on again, just long enough for him to see the six-inch length of steel gleam.

"Now you stop talking foolishment, my friend, or I swear to God I'll open you up and spill your stomach around your shoes."

"I would consider that a great favor," Sanson said huskily.

They talked to each other in rattling Spanish so fast that Sanson could catch only a word here and there.

"You talk," the man said. The knife pain was stronger, deeper. Sanson involuntarily sucked his stomach away from the point of the blade.

The anger was a long time in coming, but suddenly it throbbed behind his eyes. "I haven't the faintest damn idea what you want. I'm a newspaperman on my way to Houston. I don't know anything about any package. Now take that knife out of me or I'll feed it to you."

"Big talk. Big talk," the man muttered, but he seemed a little less positive. Again they talked together. The wallet was shoved back into the side pocket of Sanson's jacket. His car keys were taken out. He caught the words "Buick" and "rojo." So they had watched him long enough to know that his car was a red Buick parked in the *zocolo.*

"And there isn't any package in it—" Sanson started. He heard the faint swish and the adobe wall behind him seemed to explode and drive the side of his head off into the hot dark night sky. There was no sensation of falling. Just an explosiveness boiling blackness. . . .

3

IT WAS AN OLD DREAM. SHE DREAMED SHE HAD
fallen out of bed onto the cool floor and in such a way
that her head was cramped back at an awkward position
against the baseboard. It made her neck hurt.

She moaned as she awakened and her hand touched
something rounded, smooth, glossy. She opened her
stunned eyes and saw that she was naked, in an empty
bathtub.

She thought, "Diana, my girl, this must have been some
party. I hope you had a good time."

And then memory flooded back. She sat up with a great
gasp. She was dizzy and her neck throbbed with pain.
She could remember dozing off in the tepid water, and
then hard hands that gouged at her, the knowledge of
death. . . .

Diana knew that a long time had passed. It was a little
cooler now. Her body was dry. She climbed stiffly from
the tub and stood for a moment, her hands braced against
the wall, breathing deeply. She pushed herself away, nauseated with weakness, and plodded doggedly into the bedroom. It took all her strength to lift the bottom corner of
the bed and pull out the caster. She poked a finger up the
hollow metal leg and sobbed aloud as she felt the empti-
ness. She went back to the bathroom and looked at her
wristwatch. Three in the morning. Five hours had passed.
The town was still. All she could hear was a truck droning
in the distance. She went back into the bedroom and looked
at the ruined shoes, the slashed suitcases, the pictures
crooked on the walls.

She shivered. She put on pajamas, stretched out across

the bed and picked up the room phone. The sleepy desk clerk intimated by the tone of his voice that this was a hell of a time to make a long distance phone call.

She lit a cigarette, lay back and waited for the phone to ring. It took twenty minutes.

There was no sleep in his voice. The name of the town from which the call was coming had alerted him. And she sensed his anger at this violation of the rules he had made.

"George, honey? This is Diana. I just got lonesome and had to call you up."

"That's interesting."

"I had hard luck today, George. You know I planned on buying you a present down here. Well, I put the money in a special place and darn if somebody didn't steal it. Now what am I going to do?"

There was a long silence. "Maybe you were careless," he said then.

"No, George. I was real careful. It was just one of those things, I guess."

"Any idea who took it?"

"Not the slightest."

Again there was a long silence. He laughed harshly. "I'd hate to think, kid, that you just decided to spend the money on yourself instead of buying me a present."

Her hand tightened on the phone. "Gee, George, I'm not dumb enough to make you mad at me."

"I hope not. Having a good time?"

"As good as I can away from you, George. Do you still want a present?"

"It would be nice."

"You know, George, wouldn't it be funny if you told somebody that I had the money with me to buy you a present and it turned out they decided to steal it?"

"Very funny, kid. Look, I'm glad you called. A friend of mine will be down that way tomorrow or the next day I've told him to look you up."

"Who, George?"

"Christy."

"Please, George. No!"

"He's a nice guy, kid. I know you don't like him, but he's a nice guy. Show him a good time for me."

The line clicked as he hung up.

Diana walked the floor for an hour. She walked with her fists clenched and tears in the corners of her eyes. If she packed and ran, George would be sure that she had crossed him, and George had a special and unmentionable way of dealing with people like that. But if she stayed it meant Christy, and she knew from George's tone that he was angry enough with her to throw her to Christy. Christy, with his queer twisted mind. She remembered how she and George had laughed about Christy.

George had been kidding her, she had thought, when he said, "If you ever make me mad, kid, I'll hand you over to Christy."

And now, suddenly, horribly, she knew that he hadn't been joking. What a fool she had been to think that because she had lasted longer with George than any previous girl, it had been for keeps. With all her heart she wished she were back at Club Tempo, doing the five a night, whispering the bawdy lyrics into the mike, swaying with the beats of Kits Nooden's Midnight Five.

Into her mind flashed a picture of the empty eyes and broken mouth of the young girl Christy had brought down from upstate.

It had been almost a year ago that George had explained Christy to her. He had said, "Kid, I'm in the roughest, dirtiest business in the world. I got to have a guy like Christy around. I admit it makes me feel like an animal trainer sometimes, but nobody who knows me and knows Christy ever wants to cross me up."

She turned out the lights and smothered her weeping with the pillow. Maybe George had spoken out of anger. Maye he'd regret it, change his mind, call her back.

"George," she said softly into the night. "Please, George." For a long time she had thought that she was hard enough to bounce back from the blow. But now she felt like a frightened child, alone in the crawling dark.

4

LANE SANSON OPENED HIS LEFT EYE. THE right one felt clotted and stuck together. He raised trembling fingers and touched it, found that it was swollen shut, the skin around it taut and painful. It was daylight and he looked at an adobe wall inches from his face. He felt extraordinarily weak, far too weak for it to be the result of a garden-type hangover. He sensed that he was indoors. When he moved he felt and heard a rustle underneath him.

There was an evil taste in his mouth. He listened, attempting to identify an odd sound. A drip and slosh of water and then silence. Then another drip and slosh of water. It came from behind him. With enormous effort he rolled over. He was in some sort of small shed with a sloping roof. He could see the blue sky through holes in the roof.

A sturdy naked brown girl stood by a pail made of a five-gallon gasoline tin with a wire handle attached, taking a methodical bath. He stared at her with alarm. Her back was to him. In one corner was a wooden crate of clothes. In the other corner he could see, under a flat piece of metal, the red glow of coals atop a stove improvised of cinder blocks and bricks. A tin chamber pot with a florid rose painted on its side stood near the stove. The sun came through the roof holes and made golden coins on the packed dirt of the floor. The light gave the girl's skin coppery glints.

He was thinking that this was certainly one part of Mexico City where he had not been before and then he remembered that this was Piedras Chicas, the border town,

20

and he remembered vaguely a girl in a cantina, two men in an alley and a great explosion against his head. He dug down into the disjointed memories and came up with a name.

"Felicia," he said in a half-whisper.

She turned sharply. *"Bueno!"* she said. *"Momentito."* She dried herself without shyness on what appeared to be a strip of sheeting, then took a red gingham dress out of the crate and pulled it down over her head, smoothing it across her sturdy hips with the palms of her broad hands.

She came and sat beside him, cross-legged, her skirt halfway up the strong brown thighs. She leaned forward and put her hand on his forehead. *"Ai!"* she said. "Hot!"

He coughed, said in Spanish, "If you speak slowly, *chica,* I can understand. How do I come to be in this place?"

"Truly, it is like this. I was in the *zocolo.* Two men came to me and asked if I would wish to earn twenty pesos. Of a certainty, I said. They were strangers to me and their accent is of the south. They walked me to the cantina and pointed to you through the window, Lane. They promised you would not be hurt. They wished me to bring you outside to the alley and hand you over to them. It is a thing I never did before as I do not wish trouble with the *policia.* I am not a good girl, but neither am I ever taken by the *policia* and with me that is a matter of pride. They talked to you and then they hit you a great blow and came out of the alley. They gave me ten pesos and said it was enough and I spit on their feet. It appeared you were dead from the great blow and I knew that there would be much trouble. But I put my ear to your chest in the darkness and heard the poom, poom of your heart.

"You are truly heavy, Lane," she went on. "There was no one to help. But I am very strong because until last year when I became weary I worked in the fields. I dragged you through the alleys to this place, my *casita.* It is a question of pride, as they promised you would not be hurt. This, it is my fault and something I must do. There is a great wound in the side of your head, Lane. But I have prodded it with my fingers and I do not feel any looseness of the bone, so I think it is not broken. I washed it and poured in much of the dark red thing which is for bad wounds so that they do not rot. On it I have put clean cloth. This morning at dawn I lit a candle for you at the iglesia and said many small prayers. Now you wake and I shall buy food for us. See?"

She reached under the edge of the serape on which he lay and pulled out his wallet. "Nothing is gone, Lane. I am not a thief. May I take pesos for food?"

"Of course!"

She took a five-peso note and put the wallet under him. He tried to sit up and a great wave of weakness struck him. He sagged back and the flushed feeling went away. His teeth began to chatter violently.

She jumped up and brought an ancient torn blanket to cover him. He tried to grin at her. The chill grew worse.

"Pobrecito!" she said. *"Pobre gringo!"*

She pulled the blanket up and slipped in beside him. She slid one arm under his neck very gently, pulled his face into the hollow of her throat and shoulder. Her breath was warm on his cheek. She held him tightly and warmly and sang softly to him, a song without melody. The great shudders began to diminish in violence. He felt as though he were a pendulum swinging more and more slowly, as it sank with each swing further down into a restful darkness.

When next he awakened there was a flickering light of one candle in the shack. He craned his neck and stared over at her. She sat near the stove fashioning tortillas from masa, her hands slapping rhythmically. She smiled, and her eyes and teeth glinted in the candlelight.

"Tortillas con pollo. You hongry, babee?"

"And thirsty. Take some more money and get me cold beer. Two bottles. Carta Blanca or Bohemia, *por favor."*

She took the money and left. He staggered weakly across the floor and then back to his bed. His head throbbed so violently that he thought it would break open.

The icy beer made him a little tight. He wolfed down the food until she gasped in amazement. He wiped the grease from his mouth with the back of his hand and grinned over at her.

"You're a good girl, Felicia."

"Not good. I told you before. This is entirely a matter of pride."

"How many years do you have?"

"Eighteen, I think."

"Where's your family?"

Her mouth puckered up. *"Mi padre,* he drowned in the river trying to cross to the *estados unidos.* Then there is no money. The sisters, they are gone. I do not know where. *Mi madre,* she dies of the trouble in the lungs, here."

There was nothing he could answer to that.

At last his hunger was satisfied. He lay back. Sleep rolled toward him like a dark wave. Insects had found him but their tiny bites did not disturb him.

"Lane?"

"Yes, *chica.*"

"I forgot to say. Today a man was killed in the Calle Cinco de Mayo. Stabbed to the heart. It was one of the two men who talked with you in the alley and struck the great blow."

"Who is he?"

"That is not known. It is said that a tall gringo, tall like you, did that thing."

"Yes?"

"Also I heard in the market that the tall gringo is hiding somewhere in Piedras Chicas. It might be that those two thought you were he."

"That makes sense."

"What did they want of you?"

"They thought I had a package of some kind."

"Then it would appear, Lane, that the other gringo has the package."

"You are smart."

"No, it is a part of living here. This is a town of much violence, much smuggling. One learns how these things happen. It gives me to think."

"How so?"

"You came up from the south. It is said the other gringo did the same. So it is a matter of importance for him to get the package across the river, no? He hides. It is thought he has killed a man. Those who seek him and the package now know that they were mistaken in approaching you. Thus you could take the package across with perfect safety and much profit, no? They would not think you had it."

"Now wait a minute! I don't want anything to do with the police any more than you do. I'm no smuggler."

"We do not know if it is a police matter, *estupido!* Sleep, Lane. Felicia must think."

He awakened again and the shack was dark. Moonlight came through the holes in the roof. He raised his head and looked around. Felicia lay on a serape on the dirty floor, naked and asleep, her body at right angles to his, her feet near his feet.

His coat was folded under his head. He dug through the pockets and found a crumpled pack of cigarettes with one left in it. He looked at her again as he hunted for matches. Moonlight silvered her body in random patches where it shone through the holes overhead. It was a heavy, sensual body, reminding him of the island paintings of Gauguin. He put the cigarette between his lips and scratched the match. At the thin scrape of the match and the small golden flame she came awake like an animal, rolling instantly up onto her knees.

"*Ai!* she said. "You frightened me."

"Sorry, *chica.*"

She remained on her knees, looking toward him through the moonshafts. "There is one for me?"

"No. This is the last."

"I should have bought more."

The feeling of well-being that had been his during the evening after the sleep of the day was gone now. He felt dulled and aching. But the look of her moved him. "This can be shared," he said huskily.

She came to him and crouched beside him. He held the cigarette to her lips. As she inhaled the tip glowed brightly, casting a reddish glow across the broad planes of her face, the mounds of her deep breasts. He brought the cigarette to his own lips again, and then held it to hers. He put his hand on her waist tentatively, hesitantly. But his head hurt and he felt slightly nauseated. He took his hand away.

She seemed to understand at once. "You are not yet well."

"Not yet."

"It does not matter, *querido*."

She moved the serape closer to his makeshift bed and stretched out on it. He stubbed the cigarette out against the dirt floor. Her hand found his and clasped it tightly. In the night streets of the city the mongrel dogs yapped and howled. Distant roosters crowed, their throats soft and rusty with sleep. Somewhere nearby a sick child wailed. There was no light but the moon.

He awoke at dawn as Felicia came in with the stranger. The size of him dwarfed the shack. He could not stand erect in it. He was wary.

Lane found he was much stronger as he sat up and said, "Who are you?"

The man sat on his heels and offered him a pack of cigarettes. Lane took two and handed one to Felicia. The stranger lit all three gravely. "You," he said, "were the little man in the middle."

"If this busted head was supposed to be yours, where were you?"

"I wasn't in a cantina poisoning myself. This is a smart little girl you've got here."

"How long can we keep this up before somebody has to say something that means something?"

"I had a little trouble yesterday. It cramps my style, Lane. Lane. That your last name?"

"First name."

"Okay, play cute. It's contagious. Yesterday they towed your car into the courtyard of the police station. Somebody did a good job of going through it. What they left, the kids stole. But I think it still runs."

"That's nice."

"They're about to report you missing. They got the name by a cross check on the motor vehicle entry permission. I think they'll probably wait until noon."

"You get around, don't you?"

"Friends keep me informed, Lane. I've got some instructions for you. Go and get your car this morning. Get it out of that courtyard. Are your papers in order?"

"They are, but if you think I'm going to—"

"Please shut up, Lane. Get your car and drive it to a little garage at the end of Cinco de Mayo. There's a big red and yellow sign in front which says: 'Mechanico.' Tell them you want it checked over. Leave it there while you have lunch. Then get it and drive it across into Baker, Texas. Put it in the parking lot behind the Sage House. Register in the Sage House. Is that clear?"

"Damn you, I have no intention of—"

"You run off at the mouth, Lane. Damn it, how you run off! You ought to take lessons from this little girl you got. She's got a head on her. She could tell you what will happen if you don't play."

Lane looked quickly at Felicia.

"Don't bother," the stranger said. "We've been talking too fast for her to catch on. I'll give it to you straight. If you don't play ball some friends of mine are going to give the police the most careful description of you you ever heard. And they're going to tell just how you shivved that citizen yesterday. You won't get any help from the American consul on a deal like that. You'll rot in the prison in Monterrey for twenty years. Beans and tortillas, friend."

The big man smiled broadly. He was close to forty. He had a big long face, small colorless eyes and hulking shoulders. He was well dressed.

"That's a bluff," Lane Sanson said loudly.

"Ssssh!" Felicia said.

"Try me," the big man said. His tone removed the last suspicion Lane had.

"Why are you picking on me?"

"Laddy, you're still the man in the middle. Park your car behind the Sage House and leave it there. Take a look at it the next morning. That'll be tomorrow morning. If everything has gone well, laddy, there'll be a little present for you behind the sun visor on the driver's side. Then you're your own man. But if there's no present there, you'll go and see a girl named Diana Saybree—at least she'll be registered that way in the Sage House. Now memorize what you're going to say to her."

"Look, I—"

"Friend, you're in. If you don't play on the other side of the river, we have friends over there, too. This is what you say to Diana. 'Charlie says you might like to buy my car. He recommends it. You can send him a payment through the other channel. No payment, no more favors.' "

He repeated it until Lane was able to say it tonelessly after him.

The big man took a fifty-dollar bill, folded it lengthwise and laid it on the floor beside Lane's hand. "That'll cover expenses. Now go over to the police barracks as soon as they open. It's nearly six. You've got three hours."

Felicia rattled off a machine-gun burst of Spanish.

The stranger grinned. He said, "She says you can't go until she washes your clothes. It's okay by me if you don't get there until ten."

He stood up and as he ducked for the low doorway, he said, "Just follow orders and chances are by tomorrow afternoon you can be on your own way with a little dough to boot."

He was gone. Sanson's head was aching again. He rubbed the stubble on his chin. "He is not a nice man, no?" Felicia said.

"He is not a nice man, yes," answered Lane. "It is a bad thing that you should bring him here."

"That shows what you know. It was all planned by them for you to be taken by the police for the murder yesterday. Children saw you sleeping here yesterday. In the market a thing is soon made known all over town. But for me you could be in prison for murder." Her eyes flashed.

"I am truly sorry, *chica.*"

Her anger left and her smile was warm. "It is nothing."
He pushed the bill toward her. "Here. This is yours."

"No, it is much. It is more than four hundred pesos.
You see, I know the value of *dollares.* What could I do
with it? If I try to change it, the police will have me.
Better you should give me some of your pesos if you wish
to make a gift to me."

The sun was beginning to climb a hot blue sky. She
insisted that he hand over his shirt and underwear for
cleaning. He kept the blanket over him as he slipped them
off. She laughed at him and left with them in her hand.
She came back in an hour to cook for them and to tell
him that his things were drying in the sun. She heated the
tin of water over the charcoal fire and brought him his
dry clothes. His suit was badly wrinkled. He called to her
and she came in. He handed her his pesos.

She took them without looking up into his face. She
seemed suddenly shy.

"Muchas gracias, Felicia."

"It is nothing, señor."

He touched her cheek, slipped his hand under her chin
and lifted her face until he could look into the deep wild
gleam of the black eyes.

"Truly a daughter of many great kings," he whispered.

She took his hand and kissed it. "Go with God, Señor
Lane."

After lunch he walked back to the garage where he had
left the car. A small man with large sores at the corners
of his mouth charged him ten pesos for the work on the car.

To get to the bridge he had to circle the *zocolo* with
its bandstand in the center, with its paths and rows of iron
benches. Curio shops, churches and public buildings faced
the square. As he turned the corner to head along the
fourth and last side he saw two uniformed policemen armed
with rifles standing on the walk. A crowd had gathered but
they stayed well back from the policemen, staring avidly

at the crumpled form on the walk. Others came running up to join the crowd.

As Sanson drove slowly by he saw the body of the stranger who had come to Felicia's shack. His cheek rested in a spreading pool of blood and the blue flies buzzed in a cloud around his face. The skull was subtly distorted by the impact of slugs against the brain tissue. Sanson set his jaw, clamped his hands on the wheel and resisted the impulse to tramp hard on the gas.

At the Mexican end of the bridge he surrendered the tourist card which he had renewed three times during the two years in Mexico. He signed it in the presence of the guard and was waved on. In the middle of the bridge he paid the fifty-centavo toll.

At the American end a brisk man in khaki stepped forward and said, "American citizen? Where are you coming from? Please bring your luggage inside for customs inspection."

Lane made himself grin. "I wish I could. I did too much celebrating the other night. Somebody broke into my car and took everything. All they left was the car itself."

The man stared at him. "Have an accident?"

"Fell and hit my head."

"Have you got proof of citizenship?"

Lane dug out his birth certificate. "This do?"

"Fine. Now open up the trunk, please."

The man shone a flashlight around inside the trunk, then climbed into the car and looked down into the well, where the top folded.

He turned around. "I have the idea I ought to know that name. Lane Sanson."

"There was a book, six years ago. *Battalion Front.*"

The customs man grinned. "Hell, yes! I read that thing five times. I was a dough, an old infantry paddlefoot, so it meant something to me." He backed out of the car. "You haven't written something since that I missed, have you?"

"Nothing."

"Okay, that's all the red tape, Mr. Sanson. Good luck to you."

"Thanks."

He drove down into the main street of Baker. Directly ahead and on the right he saw the Sage House, a three-story frame building painted a blinding white. The entrance was dark green. He parked in front and went in. People stared at him. He was conscious of his heavy beard, the badly rumpled suit.

"I'd like a room, please," he said.

The clerk looked at him with obvious distaste. "I'll have to see if there are any vacancies."

Sanson slipped the Bank of America traveler's checks out of the inside pocket of his wallet. "While you're looking, tell your cashier I want some of these cashed. If you have a room, I want a barber sent up in thirty minutes. And I'll want a portable typewriter, and my car put in your parking lot in the rear. I have no baggage. It was stolen over in Piedras Chicas. So I'll pay you in advance."

Under the impact of the flow of imperious demands the clerk's dubious look faded away.

"As a matter of fact, I notice that we do have a pleasant room on the second floor front. It'll come to—"

"I'll take it. Send the boy up to open it up and wait for me while I cash my traveler's checks."

"Number 202, Mr.—ah—Sanson," the clerk said, reading his signature as he wrote it. "If you'll leave your keys here—"

"They're in the car."

"I'll have a typewriter sent up, sir."

"With a twenty weight bond, black record ribbon and glazed second sheets."

"Yes, sir," the clerk said, thoroughly quelled.

Once in the room, Lane threw his jacket on the bed. He stripped off his trousers and emptied the pockets onto the bureau top. He said to the boy, "Go over to the desk and write this down." The bellhop shrugged and sat down. "Waist 32, inseam 33. That's for the slacks. For the shirts, 16 collar, 34 sleeve. Buy me two pairs of slacks, gabardine if you can get them. Pale gray or natural. And two sport shirts, plain, white, short sleeves. Take my suit along and leave it to be cleaned. Fastest possible service. I want a doctor as soon as he can get up here and, exactly one hour from now, a good barber to give me a shave and haircut. Oh, yes. Get some underwear shorts and some dark socks, plain colors, three pairs, blue or green, size 12. This ought to cover it."

The bellhop scribbled some more. "Three pair shorts?"

"That'll do it. Any questions?"

"You give me a fifty. How high you want to go on the pants and shirts?"

"Fifteen for the slacks, three and a half for the shirts. With what you have left over get some fair rye. Bring up ice and soda."

"This town is dry, sir."

"It doesn't have to be the best rye."

"I'll see what I can do."

The doctor arrived when the bathtub was almost empty. He inspected the cut, sighed, rebandaged it. "If you'd called me when it happened I could have put clamps in it and it wouldn't have made as much of a scar as it's going to now. Five dollars, please."

When he came out of the bathroom the barber had spread newspapers and put a straight chair near the windows. Just as he finished the bellhop arrived, laden with packages. Lane checked the purchases and tipped the boy. Ten minutes later, as he was dressing, the typewriter arrived, the ice and soda following soon after. Lane sent the boy back for cigarettes.

When the door was shut and he was alone, Lane Sanson unwrapped the paper and rolled a sheet into the machine. He made a drink and set it near him. He lit a cigarette.

Across the top of the first sheet he typed: A Daughter of Many Kings.

He sat for a long time, sipping the drink. When the glass was empty he began to work. The words came and they were the right words. After six years, the right words. He forgot time and place and fear.

5

THE DC-3 RUN BY THE FEEDER LINE TO BAKER
was a tired old plane. Inside it had the smell and the flavor
commonly associated with old smoking cars on marginal
railroads. It had sagged and blundered its way through
storm and hail, freezing cold and blistering heat. It had
fishtailed into a thousand inferior runways. The original
motors were five changes back. The airframe was like the
uppers of a pair of shoes resoled once too often.

The bored pilot cut the corners off the standard ap-
proach pattern and slipped into the Baker strip. The tires
leaped and squealed on the cracked concrete and he cursed
it for being a weary recalcitrant old lady as he yanked it
around and taxied it over to the cinderblock terminal building. The attendants came trotting across the baked cement.
The little line prided itself on a ninety second turnaround.
The poop sheet said two off and one on at Baker.

The pilot squatted on his haunches under the wing, a
cigarette squeezed between his yellowed fingers. The co-
pilot had gone into the building for the initialing of the
manifest.

The pilot looked at the two passengers who got off. One
of them was easy. Local cattleman, from the cream-colored
Stetson right down to the hand-sewn boots. The other one
was harder to figure. The pilot decided he wasn't the sort
you'd want to strike up any casual acquaintance with.
Brute shoulders on him. Stocky bowed legs. Long arms.
Damned if he wasn't built like one of them apes. But it
wasn't an ape's face. First you might think it was a face
like a college professor's. Those rimless glasses and that

half-bald head. Some crackpot, probably. The zany little blue eyes beamed around at the world and the mouth was wide and wet-lipped, set in the kind of smile that made you think of the time the psychology class went over to the state farm and got a look at the real funny ones.

Only, the pilot decided, you wouldn't want to laugh at this one. He wasn't dressed right for the climate in that heavy dark wool suit, but you wouldn't want to laugh at him.

The two suitcases were off-loaded and the new passenger was put aboard. The pilot flipped away his cigarette and went aboard. The steps were wheeled away. The hot motors caught immediately and he goosed it a few times. He trundled old Bertha down to the end of the runway. He glanced back. The funny-looking stranger was just getting into a cab. He looked like a big dark beetle, or like a hole in the sunlight.

Inside the cab Christy leaned back. The trip from New York had been like walking across a dark room toward one of those little tinfoil wrapped chocolate buds on the far side of the room. You wanted it and you knew it was there and you were thinking about it so you didn't see anything in the room or think of anything except feeling it between your fingers and picking it up and peeling off the tinfoil and putting it in your mouth. And Christy was never without chocolate buds in his side pocket. He took one out but already the climate had gotten to it. It pulped a little between his fingers. The expression on his face made him look like a child about to cry. All the others were soft, too. He dropped them out the window of the cab. His hands were very large, hairless and very white. The network of veins under the skin had a blue-purple tint.

He thought of Diana and he thought of George. He threw his head back and laughed. It was a high gasping, whinnying sound. George was done. You could see that coming for a long time. And so, when it looked right, you gave him a push. And the push just happened to shake Diana loose, right into his hands, after looking at her so long, and taking her lip, and seeing that contempt in her eyes.

Without realizing it, he had grasped the handle on the inside of the cab door. When he remembered how she had looked at him his jaw clamped shut and he gave an almost effortless twist of his big wrist. The screws tore out of the metal and the handle came out in his hand.

The driver gave a quick look back. "Hey, what the hell!"

"It was loose."

The driver met his glance in the rear vision mirror. "Brother, that thing was on there solid and it'll cost me at least three bucks to get it fixed."

Christy hunched forward. He put his hand casually on the driver's shoulder. He smiled wetly. "I said, friend, it was loose."

"Watch whacha doin'!" the driver said shrilly.

"It was loose."

"Okay, okay. It was loose. Leggo! Are you nuts?"

Christy leaned back and laughed again. The gutless human race. Always ready to start something and always fast to back down. The best would be George. He had decided to save that until last. Maybe at the last minute George would find out why everything was going wrong lately. It was good to think of that last minute. He knew how he'd do it. Knock George out and take him down to the boat and wire a couple of cinderblocks to his ankles. Take the boat out and sit and eat chocolates until George came around. Then say, nice and easy, that it was time George joined a lot of his old buddies.

He'd hoist him over the side, hold him there with his face above water and the cinderblocks pulling hard on his legs, and listen to George beg and promise and scream and slobber. Watch his eyes go mad. Hold him there until there wasn't any man left, just a struggling animal. Hold him and think of him and Diana together and then spit in his face and let go. It would be night and the white face would be yanked down out of sight as though something from underneath had grabbed it. Maybe bubbles would come up like with the others. Then George would be down there, doing a dance in the river current, dancing right along in the chorus with all the guys who'd tried to cut a piece of the big pie and had run into Christy instead.

The cab pulled up in front of the Sage House. Christy paid him the buck and a half rate, tipped him a solemn dime, and carried his bag inside.

"You got a reservation for me," he said. "A. Christy."

"Yes, Mr. Christy."

He had hurried all the way and now he wanted to go slow. Nice and slow.

"There's a friend of mine here, I think. Miss Saybree. Is she in?"

"I believe she's in her room. Three eighteen, sir. Shall I phone her?"

"Skip it. I'll surprise her."

Nice and slow and easy. The running was over. The girl was smart. She knew what was coming, but she hadn't tried to run out on it.

He barely noticed the room they gave him. When he was alone he stretched until the great shoulders popped and crackled. This was a hell of a long way from the carny, the garish midway, the thronging marks paying their two bits to see the Mighty Christy drive spikes with his fists, bend crowbars across his shoulders, twist horseshoes until they broke in his hands. George had seen him in the carny and seen his possibilities and had jumped in with smart expensive lawyers when there was that trouble about the girl. Temporary insanity, they had called it, and had cleared him, and from then on he'd done everything George said. Up until a year ago.

He sat on the bed and wished he had some chocolate and thought about Diana. When you want something bad enough and long enough, you get it.

When the thickness in his throat and the flame behind his eyes were too much to bear, he left the room and went up the stairs to the third floor. He passed a second-floor room where a typewriter rattled busily.

He rattled his fingernails on the door panel of Room 318. "Who is it?"

"An old pal, sweetness."

She opened the door. He grinned at her. He'd almost forgotten what a very classy dish she was. She was pale and she spoke without moving her lips.

"Come on in, Christy." She walked away from him. She walked as though she were on eggs and if she stepped too hard they'd break.

He shut the door. She had gone to sit in a straight chair. She sat with her ankles and knees together, her hands folded in her lap, like a new girl at school.

Christy sat on the bed and smiled at her. "George is sore," he said.

"I didn't want to do this in the first place," she snapped.

"George figured nobody would be looking for you. Anyway, he wanted you out of town."

"Why?" she asked, white-lipped.

"You've moved. You aren't living there any more. He had your stuff packed up and put in storage. You can get the claim check from him."

"Is—is anyone—"

"You ever meet old Bill Duneen? The horse player? He died of a stroke last year. Now George and Bill were great pals. George feels a sort of obligation to look out for Bill's daughter. Cute kid. Nineteen, I'd say. You could call her a kind of protégé. Did I get the right word?"

It surprised him that she smiled . . . "If that's the case, then I can get out of here. If you don't mind, I have to pack now."

Christy picked his teeth with a blunt thumbnail. "Sweetness, it ain't quite that easy. George said to me, he said, 'Christy, you and Diana are two of the best friends I got. I'd be real hurt if you two didn't team up.' "

"He said no such thing!"

"I've always had a real yen for you, sweetness. I'd take it bad if you tried to run out. If you ran out, I'd have to go up to that jerk town you come from and see how those kid sisters of yours look. What's the name of it? Oneonta?"

"You—you dirty—"

"Ah, ah, ah! No bad words, sweetness. George just happened to mention to me where you come from. He wants us to get along."

He smiled placidly and watched the spirit slowly drain out of her. Her mouth went lax and she lowered her head.

"How come," he said, "you let some guy take the roll?"

Her head snapped up and her eyes narrowed. "How would you know it was some guy? Why not two or three, or even a woman?"

He knew he'd said the wrong thing. It confused him. When he was so confused he got a dull ache at the crown of his head. It made him angry.

"George told me he thought it was a guy."

"George never guesses at anything."

He shrugged. "Maybe he knew."

She smiled at him and he didn't like her smile. "Christy, it wouldn't be possible that you're crossing George up? I never thought of that before. He trusts you. Maybe he's wrong."

"Come over here."

The color drained out of her face. She didn't move.

"Come over here, or I'll come and get you."

She stood up as though she were eighty years old. She came to him, one slow step after another. "Closer, angel." She obeyed. He sat on the bed and looked up at her, into her expressionless face. "You need to be straight on something. You think maybe you're a person. You're not a person any more. You're a package. A thing. George gave you to me. Free and clear. Whatever I tell you to do, you do. When you don't do what I tell you, I can make you very sorry your mother ever had you. I work for George. I earned you. You're mine like my shoes, like my socks."

She did not look directly at him and she said nothing. Her face was like death.

"It won't be that bad," he said in a huskier voice. "It won't be maybe as bad as you think." He caught her wrist and yanked her close to the bed. He reached up with his free hand, caught his fingers in the neck of her dress, ripped the dress down. She gasped but he held her tightly. He stripped away her dress, bra, half-slip so that they fell torn to the floor around her and she stood pallid and naked and afraid.

"It won't be so bad," he crooned, and he began to giggle.

From far away he heard her thin voice saying, "Don't, Christy. There's something wrong in your head. Something wrong and dirty and twisted and evil—and crazy."

Outrage drowned out desire. She had used a forbidden word. You could not use that word to Christy. He yanked down on her wrist, yanked her forward into the smashing open-handed blow against her jaw. She sprawled back, her face going blank, sprawled like a boudoir doll and fell on the grass rug on her left side. She rolled completely over twice, ending up on her face, one arm cramped under her. The fall had torn one shoe off.

Christy sat breathing hard, waiting for the anger-mist to clear away from his eyes. He began to wonder if once again he had struck a woman too hard. He watched her narrowly and sighed with relief as he saw the lift of her breathing. He got up, took the key off the bureau and carefully locked the door behind him as he left.

The blue Texas dusk was settling over the land. A lurid and impossible sunset flamed in the west. Christy walked slowly down the main street to the nearest drugstore, filled with the warmth of anticipation. He bought some chocolates, looked up the tourist court number and shut himself in the phone booth.

He asked for Mr. Brown and the woman said she'd get him to the phone. In a few minutes he heard Shaymen say cautiously, "Brown speaking."

"Drop the guard, junior. This is that man."

"You just get in?"

"I've been talking to the pigeon. You did good."

"Thanks."

"You got it to turn over?"

Shaymen hesitated. "If I feel like it."

Christy's throat began to swell. "Look, Shaymen. I steered you into this. You know your fee. Let's not get coy."

"Right now I'm in the driver's seat. If I wanted to cross

you all the way, I wouldn't even be here. And the phone is
no place to talk about it."

"Drive in and pick me up, then. In front of the Texan
Theater."

"Right away."

It was almost dark by the time Shaymen pulled up in
front of the theater. The door swung open. Christy climbed
in and sat back with a sigh. "Just drive out of town a ways
and park, Shaymen."

They did not speak again until Shaymen had pulled off
the road. He offered Christy a cigarette, used the dash
lighter.

Christy chuckled. "I know you can't cross me on the
amount, Shaymen. She had George's twenty-eight thousand
bucks. And I got the second twenty-eight thousand."

"I don't like those thousand-dollar bills."

"I'll handle those. I know a guy. Now why the coy act?"

Shaymen lifted his cigarette slowly to his lips. "So you
tipped me a week in advance where she'd be staying so I
could lift the roll. You tell me a little, but not enough. I'm
not a hired man. I told you that before. You want me
working, I've got to be on the inside. Call it a partnership."

"You're a greedy guy, aren't you? It worked the way I
figured. George sent me down with cash to replace what
you took off Diana. The purchase has to go through because he needs the merchandise. Even paying double for
it he makes a nice profit once the stuff is cut. Forty kilo-
grams. That's a little over fourteen hundred ounces. The
retailers have to make their end, you know, but even so,
George clears forty bucks an ounce. There's fifty-six thousand bucks at least. Plus two times twenty-eight thousand
is a hundred and twelve thousand bucks."

Shaymen started. "Are you going to try to grab the
stuff without paying what you brought down?"

"Right. Those boys from across the line are supposed
to be rough, but the Mexican Government is cracking
down on them. George has been busy lining up a new
source. I got all the dope on that. So if this source is going

to dry up anyway, all we got to do is freeze them out and grab the stuff without paying."

"How about George? Won't they let him know they didn't get paid?"

Christy laughed his high whinnying laugh. "You kill me, Shaymen. This isn't hit and run. They may try to tell George and maybe he won't be around to listen."

Shaymen whistled. "The works, eh?"

Christy slapped his shoulder. "You and me are in, kid. We start in with a capital of a hundred and twelve thousand, with a brand new source of stuff, with the retailers in line and with George out of the way. Now give me that dough."

"It's in a safe place," Shaymen said. "Let's just leave it there, huh?"

"I don't like your attitude, Shaymen."

Shaymen flipped his cigarette out the window. "I don't care what you like and what you don't like. So far we both got twenty-eight thousand. If what you say is right, I think we'll have fifty-six thousand apiece. That makes a partnership, doesn't it?"

"I've been taking orders too long," Christy said. "From now on I'm giving orders."

"If that's the way you want it, Christy, you can kiss that twenty-eight thousand good-by."

Christy reached over and clamped his left hand on Shaymen's closed right fist. He slowly closed his hand. Shaymen made one futile, feeble effort to slam his left fist toward Christy's face but pain brought it to a faltering stop. He threw back his head and screamed like a woman.

Christy eased off on the pressure and said, "Where's the money?"

"Damn you, Christy! In my suitcase," he said sullenly.

Christy applied the pressure again. His arm and shoulder tightened and he felt, under his palm, the crisp pop of a bone. Shaymen screamed again and fell forward across the wheel, half-fainting, his weight against the horn ring. Christy pushed him back and the blare of the horn ceased.

"Tell me where," he demanded softly.

Shaymen was panting as though he had run a long distance. "All right . . . all right. I'll . . . tell you . . . it's buried under . . . third flagstone from the front door of . . . the tourist court . . . put it there at night . . ."

"You tried to lie to me, Shaymen. You tried to be a partner."

Now the mist was thick in Christy's eyes. He ground down with all his strength. Shaymen made a damp bleating sound and slumped over against the door. Christy squeezed the closed fist inside his big hand, working his fingers alternately, feeling the solidity of the fist slowly disintegrate until it felt like a sack of gravel in his hand. And then suddenly it was limp and a small crooning sound came from Christy's lips.

He let the ruined hand drop. He wiped his own hand on the upholstery. The mist receded. He took a chocolate out of his pocket, picked off the tinfoil and put it in his mouth. He sucked at it.

When his mind was made up, he pulled the unconscious Shaymen upright and broke his jaw with one smash of his clenched right fist. He got out and pulled Shaymen into the passenger's seat, went around and got behind the wheel. He drove back to Baker and then over toward the river to the Mexican settlement. There he found a sagging warehouse without lights and he turned out the car lights as he drove behind it. He stood outside the car for some time, listening. Shaymen was still breathing. Christy dragged him out of the car and stepped on his throat with the outside edge of his shoe. Shaymen's breath whistled once and stopped. He turned Shaymen's pockets inside out, emptied the wallet and threw it aside. He smudged his hands around the wheel and over the door handles.

Death of one Mr. Brown, commercial traveler.

Back in the hotel dining room Christy ate a large steak. He went to his room and napped until eleven. At half-past twelve, moving through the darkness like a shadow, he pulled up the flagstone, found the roll of bills in oilcloth under the packed dirt, dropped the stone back and melted off into the night. He was in the hotel a little after one.

He paused at the foot of the stairs leading up to the third floor. The damn fool nearby was still typing furiously. Christy thought hard of Diana, trying to reawaken his desire for her, but all he could feel was a thick tiredness. Diana would keep. He went back to his own room, bathed and lay heavy in the darkness, the last chocolate melting on his tongue as he fell asleep.

6

AT SEVEN O'CLOCK LANE SANSON WENT DOWN to the parking lot behind the hotel. He looked behind the sun visor on his side of the car. Nothing.

He walked into the lobby and inquired at the desk for Miss Saybree's room number. This was something to do quickly, to get out of the way. He had been up at six to read the manuscript. There were crudities in it, he knew, but there were also places that had the deep tones of a great bell. In it was something of the flavor of Mexico. The preoccupation with death, the sun and the dust and the ancient faces. The patience and the hopelessness. He wanted Sandy to read it. He wanted to watch her face while she read it because it was not only confession and acknowledgment, it was hope and promise.

But Sandy was forever gone. And everything he read, saw, did, touched, heard for the rest of his life would be but half an experience because it was not shared with the only one who had ever counted and would ever count.

Sandy was so much on the surface of his mind that when the tall girl with the blonde hair opened the room door and stared at him with an odd mixture of surprise and relief he couldn't think for a moment who she was and why he stood there.

It was not easier to remember while looking at her.
There was a deep illness of the soul in her black eyes. But
in the wide, soft mouth, faintly sullen, in the uptilt of her
heavy breasts and the animal curve of hip, there was a hard,
demanding savagery that made the impact of her as frank
as a quick word said in the moving darkness.

"I have a message for you."

"Come in," she said in what he knew at once was a
singer's voice. She pushed the door shut behind him.

He smiled. "I know this sounds silly. But maybe it
won't sound so silly to you."

"What is it?"

"Charlie says you might like to buy my car. He recommends it. You can send him a payment through the other
channel. No payment, no more favors."

"Sit down, please," she said.

He sat in the wicker chair. She went over and stood by
the window, her back to him. "Where is your car?" she
asked without turning.

"Behind the hotel. In the lot. I got in last night. I was
supposed to look at it this morning. If there was a present
for me behind the visor, I was to go on my way. But there
wasn't. So I suppose that whatever Charlie is selling you
is still in the car some place."

"You don't know what he's selling me?"

"I don't think I want to know."

"Then you're smart."

"I didn't expect anybody like you on the other end
of this deal."

She spun around. He noticed for the first time that the
left side of her mouth was swollen. Tears squeezed out of
her eyes. "Shut up! Please shut up! I'm trying to think."

"Pardon me," he said indignantly.

She walked over and sat on the bed. She moved list-
lessly, without spirit.

"By the way, Charlie is very dead."

"What!"

"Oh, yes. And from the protective attitude of the police
guarding his body, I rather imagine they shot him down.

That was yesterday, early in the afternoon. Got him in the back of the head, from all appearances."

The quick look of interest faded from her face. She stared at him. "You don't owe me a thing, not a damn thing, do you?"

"Not that I can think of at the moment. Why?"

"Skip it. You don't want in on this. You look decent. You know what that means? A mark. That's Christy's word for people like you." Her tone hinted of hysteria.

"A babe in the wood?" he asked gently.

"Exactly." She looked hard at him for a long moment and then stood up and came toward him. Her face had a frozen look and she walked in a way designed to show off the long, lovely lines of her body. She stopped inches from the arm of the wicker chair. She said with calculated throatiness, "But if you could help me, I wouldn't be—standoffish."

He looked her up and down very closely, very coldly. "Darling, you have been traveling with the wrong group. Go back there and sit down. If you're in trouble, I'll try to help. But not for the prize in the bottom of the package. Just because marks are like that."

She went back to the bed and sat down, her face in her hands. He realized that she was crying silently. He went over and sat beside her and put his arm around her shoulders. She leaned against him. Her body trembled.

"Okay," he whispered. "I'm a recruit. Attired in my shining armor, I'm riding to the rescue."

She laughed through her tears. "You fool!"

"Spill it."

The door swung open. Lane looked up and saw a remarkably unappealing man. He had a body like an ape's, wore rimless glasses on his white, oddly distorted face. The girl looked up at him and Lane felt her go rigid with sudden fear.

The stranger planted his feet. "Friend of yours, Diana?" he asked mildly.

"That's right."

"How'd he get in?"

"I phoned the desk last night when I got hungry. They brought up another key."

Lane kept his arm around the girl's shoulders. It was petty defiance. The stranger acted a bit uncertain.

The stranger jerked a thumb over his shoulder in the direction of the door. "Out," he said.

The girl spoke quickly. "Oh, Christy can get away with little gestures like that." She laughed nervously. "He used to be a strong man in a circus, you know. He's never gotten over it. Once he gets his hands on you, brother, you're all through."

Lane got the clear impression that the girl was warning him and yet trying to tell him something. He stood up and said matter-of-factly, "Well then, it looks as though I better shove off. By the way, Diana. That little matter we were just talking about—I haven't changed my mind, but I ought to know if your friend here is it."

"What the hell is this?" Christy demanded.

"He's it," Diana said quickly, "but I've changed my mind. Please don't."

Lane hesitated. Diana stood up, too. Christy pushed between them and shoved Diana away from him so brutally that she staggered and nearly fell. She looked up at Lane, her eyes meaningful in her white face.

"Now get out. Fast," Christy said.

Lane smiled broadly and said, "Let me get my cigarettes, if you don't mind." He had seen cigarettes on the bureau. He stepped quickly around Christy and went to the bureau. His back was to Christy. Instead of the cigarettes, he picked up the heavy glass tumbler. He glanced in the mirror and saw that Christy was looking at the girl.

He spun with the tumbler in his hand, his right arm coming up and over. He threw it at the side of Christy's head. It hit with a solid and sickening thud. The tumbler fell to the rug, bounced and rolled away. Christy stood, his eyes filled with an inward bemused expression. Lane reached him in two steps. Christy was shaking his head slowly. Lane hit him in the jaw with all his strength. Christy rocked but he didn't go down. His hands moved slowly toward Lane. As Lane sidestepped to avoid them he saw- the girl standing a little apart from them, her clenched hands between her breasts.

Lane hit Christy again and again and again. The only sound in the room was the thick, dead impact of bone on flesh. The little blue eyes were glazed and the glasses were jolted off so that they hung by one bow from the left ear. The big hands worked and there was something almost like a smile on Christy's face. He could no longer lift his arms. Lane swung and the glasses bounced away and broke on the floor. A vast pain ran up his right arm from his knuckles. He had the horrifying feeling that Christy was slowly recovering from the blow from the tumbler. Lane grunted with the effort as he swung. Christy's mouth was losing its shape. His jaw began to sag and a tiny spray of blood began to jet with each impact.

Suddenly he dropped to his knees, one hand on the bed to hold himself erect. Lane, knowing that he was too arm-weary to punch the man again, swung the side of his shoe up against the point of Christy's chin. The big head tilted back sharply. He was poised in that position for a moment, and then with a sigh he went over onto his side, tugging the spread from the bed with his left hand so that it fell across his short, stocky legs.

Lane was trembling with weakness. "Good Lord!" he gasped. "I was beginning to think he couldn't be knocked out."

The girl was taking quick, short steps in Christy's direction. He saw her foot swing back and he grabbed her just in time, before the high heel slashed the unconscious man's face. She turned into his arms, laughing and crying and trembling from head to foot.

He held her away and slapped her twice. Bright color appeared in her cheeks and the sounds stopped as though a switch had been pulled.

"We'll have to tie him. With something strong. Coat hangers ought to do it—the wire kind."

She brought a handful of hangers. Lane rolled the man onto his face and wired his wrists together behind him, then his ankles. He used three hangers on the wrists and three on the ankles, twisting all the ends tight. He soaked a hand towel, jammed most of it into Christy's mouth and then tied it in place with one of Diana's nylons.

Only then did they sit down, utterly exhausted from the physical and emotional strain. As he sat in the stupor that comes after violent action, Diana went and knelt beside Christy. He numbly watched her take a fat sheaf of large bills from an inside pocket. From another pocket she took a tight roll of bills wrapped in oilcloth and fastened with a rubber band.

She sat very still, a curious expression on her face.

"What's the matter?"

"I'm busy adding two and two."

"From here that looks like a lot of money."

"It is."

"Is that the money to pay for whatever is hidden in my car?"

"Yes."

"Would it be too much trouble to brief me? Or would you rather not?"

She smiled at him. "Maybe some day I'll be able to tell you how much I owe you." She laughed. "I don't know your name, even."

"Sanson. Lane Sanson."

"I've got a phone call to make, Lane. I don't want you to hear what I say."

"That's blunt enough." He stood up. "I'll wait in the bathroom."

"Wait until I get my party. It may take some time."

It had happened so quickly, so finally, leaving the big man grotesquely on the floor, that Sanson had a strong sense of unreality, a feeling that his violence had no relationship to actuality—indeed, that this had not happened. But it had happened, and with the realization came the knowledge that it was a commitment he did not care to make. Once an act is performed there is no handy way to sidestep the flow of events that stem from that act. The record of his failure with Sandy was a record of responsibilities sidestepped because the initial act was never performed. But with this act a strong flow of events had been initiated. He did not know where they would carry him, but he did know that with his act he had ceased to function in any way as a free agent, and thus would be carried along with the events, a reluctant passenger. And he was afraid.

He heard the murmur of Diana's voice as she placed the phone call and it seemed to come from a great distance.

She hung up the phone and turned to smile almost shyly at him. An indescribable muskiness hung about her—not something which could be scented, but was rather felt.

"Sorry?" she asked.

"I don't know how to answer that. I am and I'm not. I never did anything like this before. God, I could have killed him with that glass!"

"I would have been glad!"

"That's nice. You could have sent cookies to my cell."

She came to him and put her palms flat against his chest. She strained up against him and kissed him. Her lips had a faint sting, like candle wax drops on the back of a hand.

"Thank you again, Lane," she said.

He smiled very wryly. "Oh, it was nothing, really." She stood so close to him that he could see the dark roots of her hair where it was growing out.

She turned away. "You're a strange man, Lane Sanson."

"Do you know chess?"

"No."

"There's something called a forcing mate. Your opponent makes a series of moves and you have only one possible response to each one. After the series, you're cooked. The first in this game was when a little brown gal came up to me in a bar in Piedras Chicas. Nothing I've done since then has been on my own."

She looked from him to Christy. "Baby's awake."

The small blue eyes were open. He looked up at the two of them without expression. Diana sat on her heels in front of Christy's face. She bounced the oilskin package up and down in her hand and her voice had a hard, teasing note. "This is going to make George happy, isn't it?"

Christy didn't answer. He was curiously immobile. Lane suddenly realized that the man was straining against the twisted wire. He bent over the wrists. The hands looked bloodless. As he watched, the wire cut into the flesh of the left wrist and the blood began to flow. The wire was taut, but it didn't slip. Diana laughed.

The phone rang. She motioned to Lane and he went into the bathroom and closed the door.

7

PATTON AND RICARDO WERE ON DUTY, IN A small basement room near the boilers. It was furnished with a chair, a table, a cot, one lamp, a phone, a washstand and a jumble of recording equipment. Ricardo snored on the couch.

Patton smiled tightly as he checked the reel of tape, then he went over and shook Ricardo awake.

"This is one you should hear, I hope, Rick," Patton said.

Ricardo sat up groggily. He shook himself awake. Patton stood up and turned up the volume on the amplifier.

"Live like a coupla moles for half your life and—"

"Shh!" Patton said.

"Here is your party," the operator said.

"George! This is Diana."

"How many times do I have to tell you not to—"

"Shut up, George, please!"

"Aren't you getting a little plump for your panties, sis?"

"I've got your present, George."

"By God, you should have it! I gave Christy the money."

"Christy, my love, happens to be tied up at the moment. With wire. Know what he had in his pocket? That little item that was stolen from me. So now I've got enough to buy it twice. Doesn't that make you think, George?"

There was a long silence. The tape reel turned slowly, recording the hum on the phone wire. "Kid," George said, "maybe I jumped a little too fast. Maybe I got sore a little too easy."

"Wouldn't you say it was a little late for that? I would."

"Kid, who clobbered Christy? That's a good trick."

"A new friend. You see, George, I need new friends. Seems like I can't depend on the old ones."

"Couldn't we skip a little misunderstanding?"

"No, George. And speaking of little misunderstandings, the salesman met with a small unimportant fatal accident."

"It was expected. There's a new deal lined up."

"I don't think I like you any more, George. I don't think I like you handing me over to Christy."

"Kid, did he say that? He was lying to you, baby. Believe me. I wouldn't think of a thing like that."

"I've got a present for you, George, but maybe I'll give it to somebody else."

"Now hold on!"

"Squirm, George. Squirm nice."

"Diana, don't play games with me."

"How's your new protégé?"

"Kid, look! Here's an angle. Give me the present and keep the double fee for yourself. It's a nice wad."

She laughed. "You know what, George? I kept myself from thinking about what a foul stinking business this is just on account of you. And now I wish you were dead, George. Do you hear me? So maybe nobody will get the present."

"Hello! Hello! Diana!" He rattled the hook. "Diana!"

There was a sharp click and that was all.

Patton picked the tape reel tenderly from the spindle and kissed it. "I love you, I love you," he said.

Ricardo had already picked up the direct line and was making his report. "Yes, sir. That's what the Saybree girl said. I can't help what Tomkinton reported. He must have missed the transfer. That's right, sir. She's got it. Well, if she hasn't gone out, she has to be calling from the hotel, doesn't she? So that's where Christy is." Ricardo listened for a long time, unconsciously nodding as though his superior were talking face to face to him. "Right away, sir," he said and hung up.

"Something new?" Patton asked.

"Tomkinton sent Clavna over this morning to look at some guy that got it during the night. Turns out it was an old friend of ours. Shaymen. Traveling under the name of Brown. Now that other phone call makes sense—the call when the girl reported the dough had been lifted.

"Christy must have sent Shaymen on ahead," Ricardo explained. "He lifted the dough and then, for some damn fool reason, Christy must have killed him, because the body looks like Christy's handiwork. We got word from our friends south of the border that they cleaned up the whole mob down there, but couldn't find any sign of the last shipment. They got it across somehow. They're going to flash Tomkinton and Clavna to pick up the little tea-party down there. I got to take the tape over. A car's on the way to grab George."

Patton grinned. "End of the road. Boy, I'm going to rent me a cellar apartment. I won't feel at home, living above ground."

"After the pinch, Pat, and after we report, would you be morally or ethically opposed to an evening of fermented juices, females of the opposite sex, and some nostalgic cantos?"

"I'm your boy."

Ricardo opened the door. "I just happen to know a nice cellar bar . . ."

He dodged out as Patton snapped his cigarette at him.

As the door closed Patton heard the warning dial tone. He shrugged and slipped a new reel on the spindle. Odds were against any last-minute information, but you couldn't be sure.

"Yes?"

"Al? This is George. I got to make a quick trip. Think you can hold the fort?"

"Maybe nobody's told you, George, but without any merchandise there won't be any fort to hold."

"That's all set. And you've got too much mouth over the phone, Al. Now get me a plane reservation to Houston and—hold on a minute. Somebody at the door. Hey, get the door for me, delicious, I'm on the phone. And look, Al, I want to get down there no later than—"

Patton grinned and whispered, "Son, you ain't goin' no place nohow."

There was a mumble of voices and then he heard George say, his voice pitched high, "But there's some mistake!" There was a click on the line.

"George!" Al said sharply. "Hey, George! What happened? George!"

A heavy voice came faintly over the line. "You can hang up now, Al. George'll be busy for a long, long time."

There was the clatter of the phone dropping from Al's hand, several hoarse grunts, a scuffling sound, a padded blow and a moan. The phone was quietly replaced on the cradle.

Patton grinned with delight. He made a quick movement and changed the equipment over so that he could use the hand mike to record. He put it right into the same tape after that last conversation.

"And thus, friends, we bring to a close this concluding episode of our exciting drama entitled 'The Snow Birds' or, 'Georgie Porgie goes to Atlanta.' This thrilling series has come to you through the courtesy of the Narcotics Division. Run, do not walk, to your nearest recruiting station and some day soon you, too, can live in a cellar."

It was all right. If the office thought it was unfunny, they could erase it from the tape. Only one thing left to do now. Grab Christy and the gal. The retailers were being picked up in droves by now. Too bad about the gal.

Nice husky voice. A looker, too. But that's what happens to little girls who run with the wrong crowd. A couple of years of that starchy prison food and nobody'd look twice at her. They sure spread once they're on the inside.

The phone rang and he grabbed it. "Yes, sir. Yes, I'll unhook and pack up the stuff. About an hour and a half. Yes, I got one more. Just George calling Al and asking him to get him a plane ticket. The pinch came right in the middle of the conversation. Thanks a lot. Good-by."

He hung up and, whistling softly, began to unhook the apparatus.

"What!" Lane Sanson said to Diana.

She held his hand with both of hers. "I can't stay here! And I can't tell you why now, but I can't have the police take him. I have to go with you. Please."

He looked at her. Christy had stopped struggling against the wire. He followed them with his eyes.

"I'll pay you, Lane. I'll pay you well."

"That's nice, but it isn't important. If there's something you have to run from, can't you do your own running? I'm up to my neck in this, but that doesn't mean I wouldn't like out. I've got a job to go to. I'm scared of the job, afraid I can't handle it. And that's enough to worry about."

"Please," she said.

"No, thanks. I'm afraid even to think of what was hidden in my car. I want it out of there. And then I want to say good-by."

Her face changed. "Okay then. But you can do a little bit, can't you?" He nodded. "Then wait here while I pack. I don't want to be left alone with him. I'll come down to your room while you pack. We'll both check out. We can leave separately so nobody will think of us as being together. I can pack what I need into one bag and leave the other here. I'll tell you the rest where he can't hear us. It won't be much for you to do."

"I'll go along with you that far, Diana."

She took fresh clothes into the bathroom and changed

quickly. She seemed to grow more nervous as she packed. She neither spoke to nor looked at Christy as they left the room. Lane told her his room number and went ahead and unlocked the door, leaving it ajar. She came in behind him as he started to pack.

"Look, my suit isn't back from the cleaners yet."

"I'll pay you for one twice as good."

He shrugged. He put the new manuscript in the bottom of the replacement suitcase he had bought when he had gone down to eat the evening before. She stood near the door. It was open a few inches.

"Where do you want me to—"

"Sssh!" she said. He looked at her in surprise. Her body was tense and she stared out at the hallway. He came quietly up behind her. Three men were just heading up to the third floor. One of them wore a ranger's uniform.

"What is it?" Lane asked in a low tone.

"We've got to get out of here."

"Now look, honey. Let's just say *you* have to get out of here. I think I'd welcome a nice warm friendly cop at this point."

She turned on him. Her face had gone feline. "You would, eh? Listen, friend. They'll grab me and you and your car. They know where you came from. And there's no power in the world that'll keep you from doing time for it."

"I've done nothing wrong."

"No? Lane, there's fourteen hundred ounces of heroin in your car. Refined diacetyl-morphine worth a quarter of a million dollars in the retail market, and you brought it in from Mexico. Do you still want to play innocent?"

"But you could explain how I happened to—"

"Either I get help from you right now or what I'll tell them about you will be something you won't want to hear."

"That's a filthy trick!"

"I'm not what you'd call a good girl, Lane."

"Somebody else said that to me a few days ago. She's worth fifty of you."

"Do you help me?"

"Just until I can get that damn stuff out of my car."

"Come on, then." She ran ahead of him down the corridor: She yanked open a broom closet, shoved her suitcase inside, and slammed the door. The back window was open. The outside fire escape reached down to the yard behind the hotel.

Diana looked out cautiously. "Okay. Come on." She went down first. He followed her. A kitchen helper stood out by the garbage cans, a cigarette between his fingers, his mouth open in surprise.

"Which one?" she said.

"Over there. The red Buick."

They both ran to it. He threw his bag into the back seat, slid behind the wheel. She jumped in beside him and slammed the door. He fumbled with the key, got the motor started and stalled it.

"Come on! Come on!" she said.

The back tires skidded and threw gravel. He drove down the alley beside the hotel. Evidently the kitchen helper had run in to the desk. The clerk came along the sidewalk, his face red and angry. He jumped into the alley mouth, blocking the way, and stood there waving his arms.

Lane lifted his foot from the gas. Diana reached her foot over and trod down on his. The car leaped forward. The clerk made a frantic dive for his life. Lane got a quick glance at the man rolling over and over on the sidewalk as they shot out into the traffic. He wrenched the wheel hard to avoid a big truck. The tires screamed, horns blew, and people shouted angrily at him.

The midmorning sun beat hotly down on the town.

"Now slow and easy," Diana said.

"Oh, fine," he said bitterly.

"Head east out of town. Step it up once you're outside the city limits."

"Yessir, boss."

He stepped it up to seventy. The two-lane concrete rushed at them and was whipped under the wheels.

"Can't you make it faster?"

"Take a look at the heat gauge, boss. The radiator needs flushing. Any faster and I burn up the motor."

They sped through country full of reddish stone, cactus and sparse dry grass. Far ahead the road disappeared into the shimmer of heat waves.

After a full hour in which neither of them spoke, Lane saw a side road far ahead. It led over to a grove of live oaks that were livid green in the sunbaked expanse. It was a dirt road and he could only hope that the live oaks did not screen a house.

He stepped hard on the brakes, corrected a tendency to skid, and shot down the dirt road, the car bouncing high.

"What are you doing?" she shouted.

"Shut up, angel. There's been a shift of authority. You've been deposed."

She tried to grab the wheel. He slapped her hand away. The road turned sharply to the left once it reached the grove. A dry creek bed ran through the grove. There was no house. He pulled the car under the biggest tree and cut off the motor.

"What kind of a bright idea is this?"

"Please shut up." He took the keys out of the switch and put them in his pocket. The world seemed silent after the roar of the motor. In the distance a mourning dove cried softly. On the highway three hundred yards away a car sped by with an odd whistling drone, fading off into the distance.

He unlocked the back end and took out a screwdriver and an adjustable wrench.

"Would you know where they hide stuff on a car?"

She didn't answer him. He shrugged, released the hood catch and shoved the hood up. The wave of motor heat struck him. He stared at the motor for a time. He didn't know the characteristics of the drug, but he imagined it was a crystalline substance. Motor heat wouldn't do it much good probably. It was probably somewhere in the body of the car.

He told her to get out of the car. She didn't move, didn't look at him. He took her wrist and pulled her out. She walked woodenly over to a patch of grass under one of the trees and sat down with her back to him.

Lane began to sweat from exertion as he yanked the seats out. He examined them carefully but could see no evidence that they had been tampered with. Then he lay on his back and peered up under the dash.

It took him an hour to find the answer. The simplicity of it made him angry. They had merely removed the inside panel from the left-hand door. The long sausage-like package wrapped in pale yellow oilskin was against the bottom of the door below the window mechanism. He took it out and held it, trying to guess its weight. Close to ten pounds. Nine, probably. He remembered the figure for the number of grains in a pound. Seven thousand sixteen. Nine pounds would be about sixty-three thousand grains. That would mean about four dollars a grain retail to the addict, if the girl hadn't lied to him about its value.

He put the package aside and replaced the panel, then put the seats back in. He tossed the package onto the front seat, went over to Diana and offered her a cigarette. She took it silently and he lit hers and his own. He sat down near her.

"Now I'll tell you why this was a damn fool stunt," he said.

"Don't strain yourself."

"In the first place, it's easy to recognize the car. Look over at the plates."

She looked. "Why, they're out of date!"

"Sure they are. It doesn't make any difference in Mexico. I was going to buy Texas plates. That makes the car stand out like a sore thumb. How far could we get? Do you think the hotel hasn't given the cops that license number? I wrote it on the register when I checked in. Now here's the second pitch. In this area either you're on the main roads or you're a dead duck. The secondary roads just aren't there. It makes it awfully easy to block off a whole area. If we'd kept going, we wouldn't have gotten out. Radio goes a lot faster than my red wagon."

"What can we do?" she asked hopelessly.

"I've been giving that a lot of thought. I forgot about a witness across the border who can clear me. I was all kinds of a damn fool to let you stampede me into running. Running is always the worst thing you can do. I know. I've done too much running in the past. This is my first experience running from the law, though."

"Do you expect me to go back there?"

"How can I say that? Lady, I don't even know what your problems are. All I know about you is that you were in trouble, that in a weak moment I helped you out, that you're mixed up in what I think is the most vicious business in the world, and that when the squeeze came you dropped your Lorelei role and switched to blackmail. That covers the information. The only other thing I know about you is that you're probably the most provocative-looking item I've ever seen in my life."

"You say such sweet things."

"I'm going to wait for dark and then I'm going back to Baker. You can do whatever you want—come with me, stay here, hitch-hike, or drop dead. I want to get all the way back into town and into the hotel before being stopped. That's the only way I can clear myself of running out on a hotel bill. Then I'm turning that package over to the law and telling them everything I know."

"No, Lane. No, please."

He pushed her hand away. "No more of that, sugar. It doesn't work any more."

She grew as solemn as a child. "But I have to get to New York with that package. While you were driving I was planning on what I would do, too. You see, it won't do any good for me to be picked up and for that package to be taken. It won't stop anything or cure anything. There's a man in New York. I want to go to him. And I want to make a phone call so that after I take that package to him they'll come for him and find it there. He laughs about them. They've been trying to get him for years. But he's clever."

"Then," said Lane, "Little Lord Fauntleroy told the fairy

princess that he believed every last word that dripped from her dainty lips."

"It's the truth!"

He lay back and locked his hands behind his head. He squinted up at the blue sky through the live oak leaves. "Darling," he said lazily, "I wouldn't believe you if you were on your deathbed and I were your only child."

She called him a short name. He turned and grinned at her. "Now you're in character again."

Tears filled her eyes and overflowed down her cheeks. She said in a small voice, "I'll tell you a story. I suppose it's a pretty common one. I wouldn't know. It isn't a pretty story and it has the corniest possible beginning. It started five years ago in one of those little upstate New York towns, the ones with the elms and the white houses. When I say corny, Lane, I really mean it. I sang in the church choir."

He turned up onto one elbow. "Oh, come now!" But he looked at her face and knew that she was telling the truth.

"You know how it is," she said. "You're full of wanting and wanting and yet you don't really know exactly what it is you want or how to go about getting it. Everything seems dull and you keep imagining yourself as a movie actress or something. Everybody says you're pretty. I was a brunette then. And you think of the kind of man you want, and all of them in the town that aren't married, they seem so young and dumb. Nothing to them.

"Then a band came to town to play for a big dance, I went with a boy and there was a fellow in the band. He played a trumpet. Whenever I was on the floor I could feel him watching me. When I looked at him it was as though we shared some kind of secret we couldn't talk about. It made me crazy to find out what the secret was. Oh, he wasn't good-looking. He was nearly bald and he wasn't tall, but there was something about him.

"When the band left I followed them, on a coach. It was like that. They let me sing with them and they didn't pay much because I was green and I had a lot to learn. When we were in New York the regular girl singer who had been sick came back to work. I couldn't go home then.

It was too late to go home. The trumpet player went with another band and they went out to the coast and I didn't have enough money to follow them. I guess he didn't want me to, anyway.

"You learn a lot when you have to learn fast. And the biggest thing I learned was that my voice was really no good. No good at all. That's a hard thing to learn, Lane. Then George came along. He was the sort of man I'd dreamed about back in the small town. Tall and dark, with a nice crooked smile. He could order wines and he drove a big car and everybody gave him a table as soon as he went into a place. When it was too late I found out what kind of business he was in. By then I couldn't leave him. And just the other day I found out that there isn't any goodness in him at all. Nothing but cruelty. Now I want to hurt him."

"This George," Lane said, "he sent you down here to pick up that package? Why?"

"He's been a little worried for a long time. He was afraid that one of the regular people might be trapped by the law. He thought they might not think I'd be trusted for a thing like this. But George knew he could trust me. Then somehow Christy, who works for him, had someone steal the money I was going to use to pay for it. Then George was angry and he had to send Christy down with more money. I knew that George was getting tired of me, but I wouldn't admit it to myself. So he told Christy that he wasn't interested any more and he could have me if he wanted."

"Wouldn't that be up to you?"

"Not in George's crowd, Lane. Not in a group working outside the law like they do. The rules are different. Now do you believe me when I tell you that all I want to do is frame George? I don't care what happens after that."

Lane Sanson shut his eyes against the sun glare. He could hear the soft metronome of her weeping.

"There's a better way," he said. "We'll both go back and you tell those people what you want to do. Let them rig it for you. If they want the goods on this George character, they'll play ball with you."

"They won't trust me," she said in a small voice.

"That's a chance you have to take."

"I'm frightened, Lane."

"Of what?"

"Prison. I dream of it sometimes. All gray walls and gray cotton and it's always raining and big bells ringing. Do this, do that. Years and years, Lane."

She flung herself toward him, her weight against his chest, her head under his chin, and the sobs shook her and her tears scalded his throat. He put his arm around her and tried to comfort her.

When at last the tempo of the sobs decreased until they were only great shuddering breaths that came at long intervals, he said, "So we'll go back as soon as it's dark?"

Her voice was muffled. "Anything you say, Lane."

"To keep you amused," he said bitterly, "I shall now tell you a long story of a promising young citizen named Lane Sanson who, as far as reports go, apparently dropped dead several years ago. It is a long amusing story about a book and a blonde wife and a problem involving integrity."

"Tell me," she whispered.

8

WHEN TOMKINTON, CLAVNA AND THE RANGER, who was named Vance, came into the third-floor room all Christy could do was look at them with his small alert blue eyes.

Tomkinton came quickly back from the bathroom. He

checked the top drawers of the bureau. He whistled softly. "Bad, bad news, Clav. The bird has flown."

Clavna cursed with great feeling. "Oh, that's fine! That's great! We can probably get jobs as ribbon clerks. You had to be the one to say we didn't have to cover the whole joint because there was no reason for her to run."

"Don't try to pass the buck to me," Tomkinton said hotly.

"No need to get in a fuss," Vance said. "This is a tough town to run away from. I'll put the lid on." He picked up the room phone.

As he picked it up there was a loud scream of rubber in front of the hotel. Tomkinton ran to the window. A red Buick convertible, several years old, rocked down through traffic. He squinted but the car was too far away for him to read the license.

"Go down to the lobby and see what you can find out, Clav," he directed.

Vance, on the phone, was saying, "You already got the description. The Saybree woman. Yeah. Give them the word at the bridge and tell Hal that I think's it's hot enough to radio up the line for the usual road block. That leaves the airport and the bus station."

He hung up and grinned at Tomkinton. He was a lean man with a saddle-leather face and the ranger uniform sat well on his shoulders. "Least we got us a murderer if you boys got the right dope on this guy on the floor. He is the one you called Christy, isn't he?"

"That's him," Tomkinton said. Tomkinton was a young, round-faced man with the look of an affable bank teller. He walked over to Christy. He said softly, "Killing Shaymen was a mistake, friend. A bad mistake. Not up to your usual style."

He took out his knife and cut the nylon. He yanked the towel from Christy's mouth. It was stained with blood where it had touched Christy's lips. Christy coughed and moistened his lips with his tongue. "My wrists are killing me," he muttered.

"Where did the girl go?"

"I don't know. She left with a guy. Tall fella with a little bandage on his head. I never saw him before. . . . The two of them busted me with a glass when I wasn't looking. How about these wrists?"

Clavna trotted through the open door. "Hey, she left with a guy named Lane Sanson. He had a room on the second floor. They went down the fire escape and took off in a red Buick convertible. Here's the license number. I wrote it down."

Vance took the slip of paper and picked up the phone again. As he waited he said, "This'll make it easier."

Tomkinton frowned. "Lane Sanson. Lane Sanson. I've heard that name before. Wait a minute. Newspaper guy. War correspondent. Hey, he wrote a book! I saw the movie."

Vance was talking softly over the phone. Clavna grinned. "A newspaper screwball. Boy, that's all we need. What the hell do you think he thought he was doing to leave here with the Saybree woman?"

"Maybe chivalry isn't dead," Tomkinton said.

"He'll get chivalried, all right," Clavna said, his thin dark face alight with wry amusement. "He'll get a bellyful."

"Especially if they have the junk with them," Tomkinton said.

Vance hung up. "All over but the shouting," he said. "That car'll be grabbed within two hours unless it sprouts wings. Already they got a report that it's heading east."

"How about taking this wire off me?" Christy whined.

Tomkinton knelt by him and untwisted the wire around his ankles first. Christy sighed and worked his thick legs. Finally the wrists were free. Christy got onto his hands and knees, then lumbered up onto his feet. He massaged his big white hands, inspected the wire cuts on his wrists.

"You guys are confusing me, talking about Shaymen," he said. "I know the guy. I saw him in New York maybe three weeks ago. If somebody bumped him, it wasn't me."

"You killed him last night," Tomkinton said.

"Nuts!" Last night I was here, in Texas. How could I kill a guy in New York?"

"You killed him here."

Christy looked at Tomkinton with blank amazement. "Here? Shaymen here? Well, I'll be damned! What do you suppose he was doing here? Spying on me or something?"

"What did you come here for, Christy?" Clavna asked. "As if we didn't know."

"Well, boys, it's like this. Miss Saybree run out on the boss. He was worried about her. He found out she was here. So he sent me down to talk her into coming back. He couldn't get away himself. You know how it is."

"He won't be getting away for some time," Clavna said.

Christy was motionless for long seconds. "What do you mean by that?" he asked in a low voice.

"You should keep up on these things, Christy," Tomkinton said, smiling cheerfully. "The whole crew has been picked up. George, Al, Denny, Myron, Looba, Stace. Every one of them. And this isn't just one of those suspicious deals. This is the works. Right down the line. They haven't got a million to one chance of squeaking out. And neither have you. We'll let the State of Texas take care of you for the murder, though. That'll be the simplest, cleanest way."

"I don't know anything about no murder," Christy said.

"Not even," Tomkinton said, "with Clavna here tailing you and seeing you get picked up in front of a movie house in a car and noting down the license number and then Vance telling us it was Shaymen's car, found this morning with his body beside it?"

Vance jingled the cuffs. He walked over to Christy. "Hold 'em out," he said calmly.

Christy numbly stuck his big hands out. Vance started to snap the open cuffs down on the thick wrists. Christy's hands flicked wide apart, then clamped down onto Vance's wrists. The white, wet-lipped face had gone completely mad. He flung Vance at Clavna like an awkward doll. The flying body smashed Clavna against the wall and, as they slid down in a heap, Christy reached Tomkinton in one bearlike bound.

Tomkinton was trying to scuttle backward and snatch the Police Positive from its awkward place in his right hip pocket at the same time. As he yanked it free, tearing the pocket, Christy's right fist clubbed against the side of his head like an oak knot. The blow that knocked Tomkinton cleanly through the open bathroom door and sent him sliding across the tile to stop against the tub, fractured consciousness the way a piece of string is broken.

Vance, prone across the legs of the unconscious Clavna, was groggily shifting his revolver to his left hand, having found that there was no life in the right one. He fired once as he saw the heavy shoes swinging toward his eyes, swinging in slow motion, blotting out all the light in the world.

The slug tore through the top of Christy's right shoulder, just above the collarbone. As an after-echo of the shot he heard it smack into the wall behind him. A warmth and wetness ran down his chest and his back under the dark wool suit coat. It drove him back a half-step. His right arm was still functioning. He snatched up the revolver from beside Vance's hand and stuffed it inside his belt. He had never carried or used a gun. It always made him feel weak and sick even to look at one.

He opened the door and ran out into the hall. He was halfway down to the second floor when he heard steps coming along the second floor to the stairway—running steps.

Christy turned and stared up at the third floor. As the steps came up behind him he said excitedly, "I heard a shot up there!"

The ranger ran by him without a word. Christy turned and went down to the second floor, then down the next flight. He slowed as he reached the lobby. He walked out the front door onto the sidewalk. A state police car was parked near the entrance. It was empty and the door was open.

Christy walked steadily down toward the bridge. The midmorning sun was hot on the back of his neck. He could feel his shirt sticking to him.

He made himself smile and nod at the U.S. officials. "Just going over for a coupla hours," he called.

The man waved him on. He paid the pedestrian toll to the Mexican guard in the middle of the bridge. The sun was a hot weight behind him, pushing him along. He touched his shirt pocket and felt the crispness of the bills he had taken from Shaymen's billfold. Not much, but maybe it would be enough.

The guards at the Mexican end were checking cars as he walked by. They paid no attention to him. Barefooted women sat on the sidewalk, their backs against the wall, little piles of fruit and eggs in front of them. Christy felt weak. The blood soaked his right side at the waistline. A half-block from the public square on the opposite side from the bridge he saw the sign. He climbed the dark stairway. There was one man in the waiting room. The nurse was a cute little thing in starched white. She spoke to him in rapid Spanish.

Christy sighed and took the revolver out. The waiting patient's eyes widened and he crossed himself. The nurse gave a little cry of fear. He motioned them both toward the other door. The nurse opened it and backed in. The man slipped around her. The doctor looked up with sharp annoyance from the boy whose infected leg he was treating. His eyes narrowed as he saw the gun but the expression of annoyance remained on his slim olive face.

"What do you want?" the doctor snapped.

"I'm shot. I want help."

"Put the gun away."

"Nuts. Tell the kid and the man and your nurse to go over into that corner and face the wall and keep their mouths shut. Hurry it up."

The doctor spoke to the three. They meekly did as they were told. Christy put the gun in his left hand, shrugged his right arm out of the coat. He unbuttoned his shirt, pulled the cloth away from the wound and got his right arm out of the sleeve. Then he transferred the gun to his right hand and got his left arm out of the coat and shirt. He dropped them to the floor. The doctor watched him calmly.

Christy said, "Now fix me up, Doc. That's a pretty little nurse. You try anything funny with me and I shoot her right in the small of the back."

"You are a stupid man, señor. I can work easier if you sit down. There."

"Is it bad?"

"No. It tore the muscle very little. Hit no bone. Hold still."

Antiseptic burned through the wound. Christy sucked in his breath sharply. The doctor applied folded bandages to the entrance wound and the exit wound and bound them tightly in place with gauze, wrapping it over the shoulder, under the armpit and around the great chest. He anchored the bandages more securely in place with wide strips of adhesive.

"Done," the doctor said.

"Now have the girl wash out my shirt in that sink over there and wring it as dry as she can get it." He took the money from the shirt pocket and threw the garment toward the girl. She did as she was directed. The doctor spoke to the boy and he came timidly over. The doctor began to finish his work on the infected leg while the boy watched the gun with wide eyes.

Christy put the damp white shirt on, then the coat. The doctor looked up. "That will be twenty American dollars, señor."

Christy laughed. "You make good jokes."

The doctor turned white around the mouth. "That is my profession and I get paid for my profession, señor. Pay me or I shall go to that window and call to the police." The dark eyes looked at Christy with contempt, without fear.

"Are you completely nuts?"

The doctor turned his back on the gun and walked steadily to the window.

"All right, all right," Christy shouted. He threw two tens on the floor. The doctor spoke to the nurse. She picked them up and handed them to him.

"Do you want a receipt, señor?" the doctor asked, amusement in his eyes.

"No," Christy said thickly. He hurried out. In the waiting room he turned and called back, "None of you leave here for a half hour."

The doctor and the nurse turned and stared at him as though he had already been forgotten. The nurse handed the doctor a roll of adhesive tape and he once again bent over the infected leg.

Halfway down the stairway, Christy stopped and tried to plan the next move. It would be wise to wait until midnight. In some bar he could find a tourist. The tourist would have a car. A car would get him to Vera Cruz or Tampico. Somehow he would get on a ship. He wondered if he'd killed the ranger. The man had slumped with his head at a funny angle. Soon they'd check up and find he'd crossed the bridge. They'd be looking for him. The Piedras Chicas police would be looking. They'd have his description.

He turned down another side street. It was empty. He found a barred wooden door set into a cement wall. He got his thick fingers around the edge of it, braced his feet and wrenched it open, hearing the squeal as the nails tore free. He went inside and pushed the door shut. He was in a quiet garden patio. He stood and listened. He fitted the nails back into the holes, wrapped a handkerchief around his knuckles and drove them in. Again he listened. A small fountain tinkled in the middle of the patio. Christy crawled back into a place where the shrubbery was dense. He lay down with his back against the wall. The torn shoulder throbbed.

After an hour had passed a stocky blonde woman with a ravaged face came out to the flagstones near the fountain. Christy watched her from the shadows. She spread a blanket, went back toward the house, and returned a few minutes later with a tall bottle and a tiny glass. She slipped out of her housecoat and lay face down under the brute sun.

9

IT WAS BLUE DUSK WHEN HE AWOKE. HE SAT
up with a start, feeling for the keys in his pocket as he
turned, feeling the keys at the same instant he saw the car,
as he saw Diana sleeping beside him. He exhaled slowly.
There was a tang of burning cedar scrub in the air and he
heard the distant tank-tankle of goat bells.

Sleep had ironed out the torment in her face, so that
she looked almost childlike. She lay on her left side, facing
him, both hands with the palms together under her cheek.
A thick rope of blonde hair lay forward across her throat.
Her knees were bent and thrust forward toward him. The
line of her waist dipped sharply inward and then mounted
high over the round crest of hip. He lit a cigarette and
watched her in the gathering darkness as he smoked, thinking that few things in the world are more beautiful than the
line of hip and flank of a sleeping woman.

His watched had stopped at four. The car clock would
still be operating. Soon it would be time to turn back to
town. He wondered if he had made a mistake in not in-
sisting that they turn back as soon as she had agreed that
it was the thing to do. But if they had been picked up on
the road, it might have appeared that they were doubling
back, still in flight. Darkness would give them a good
chance to reach the hotel without being stopped.

He wondered if Diana could go free by giving evidence.
He hoped so.

She began to make small crying sounds in her sleep. Her
shoulder twitched. He butted his cigarette against the trunk

69

of the tree and kissed her on the lips. She awoke with a start and a frightened cry.

"Oh, Lane!" she said. "I was frightened. I was running and running and the ground was going by under my feet, carrying me backward no matter how hard I ran. And Christy was standing and grinning and waiting for me."

"We've got to go, kitten."

She stood up and smoothed her dress down with the palms of her hands. "Gee, I'm messy," she said.

"Still think I'm wrong to take you back?"

He stood beside her. She smiled up into his face. "You gave me a chance to make that decision. I watched you while you slept. There was the car and I knew the keys were in your pocket. There was even a rock. See it over there? As big as a baseball. If I hadn't decided you were right, you'd have a terrible headache by now, Lane."

"A little too trusting of me to go to sleep, wasn't it?"

"Maybe that's why I couldn't hit you."

He looked through the night toward the west and sighed. "I guess we better go get this over with."

She stood close to him, wrapped her thin fingers around his wrist. Her fingers were cold. "I watched you while you were sleeping," she said in a half-whisper. "It should have been you, Lane. Somebody like you. Right from the start. I kept pretending that was the way it was."

She seemed so forlorn and small and lost. He put his arm around her. She put her face against his shoulder, blonde hair touching the side of his jaw. She lifted her mouth and he kissed her.

Without his knowing precisely how it happened, they were both down on the dark ground again. Her breath was like a quick furnace, her mouth like broken flowers, her body flexing, adjusting itself to him, eagerly awaiting and accepting him. Suddenly he remembered the daughter of many kings, and the silver blots of moonlight on her. And remembered back further, back to the slender ease of Sandy, and the long Sunday mornings.

He forced himself away from the girl. He stood up.

"It's no good," she said in a clear, bitter voice. "No damn good. Too many others. That's it, isn't it?"

"No. That isn't it."

She began to weep helplessly. He helped her up. They got into the car. He started it, turned the lights on, headed west. The sound of weeping ceased after a time.

Finally she said, in a clear, questioning tone, "You know something? I'm going back into trouble. But I feel good, Lane. I feel excited, as though I were going to my first dance. Why is that?"

"Relief, maybe. You've been afraid and you've felt guilty. Now the decision is made and you aren't afraid any more."

"Is it that simple?"

"Why not?"

"Maybe part of it is you, Lane."

He frowned at her in the dimness of the dash light. "How so?"

She was looking straight at the road. "Maybe I love you."

"You don't. You shouldn't. It can't work."

"Sandy?"

"I guess so. One-woman man."

"I guessed that might be what it was that . . . stopped you. Back there. But, oh, Lane, let's be gay for now. Let's pretend we're going to a dance or something."

"With a good band. And refreshments in a tent."

"No square dances, though."

"If they have any, we'll sit them out."

She moved close and leaned her head on his shoulder. She sang all the rest of the way. The old, good songs. Her voice was small, husky and true. He had the feeling that she was singing not to him but to the past and that this was, for her, a sort of farewell. Then there were the lights of Baker ahead, the neon on the tourist courts, the cars flanked outside the drive-ins, the floodlights on the river bridge. As soon as they were in the town she moved away from him, sat huddled and silent.

He parked a hundred feet beyond the hotel entrance. The space was short and it took him a long time to work the car in next to the curb.

"You stay right here," he said. "Let me handle it."

He had by habit taken the keys from the ignition. He saw her looking at him. Beyond her he could see through the open door of a drugstore. It all looked so completely sane and ordinary that for the passing of several seconds he had the feeling that all this was a masquerade of some sort, that there was no truth in what Diana had told him, that it was a cleverly planned fantasy and any moment now a group of friends from the old days would leap from the shadows, laughing, confessing, explaining.

He threw the keys over into her lap, got out and chunked the door shut. He walked with long strides to the hotel entrance and, with his head high, he went in, wearing what he fervently hoped was a confident and optimistic smile.

At dusk the chunky blonde woman stood up and pulled on her housecoat. During the long afternoon she had repeatedly filled the small glass and drank. Christy was tortured with thirst. And there was a new fear in him. His shoulder felt hot and swollen now and the pulsing was worse. He had felt the heat creep up from the base of his neck, flushing his right cheek, extending the throb to his heavy jawbone and his right ear. It was hard to remember just where he was and why he was hiding. He would remember perfectly, and then there would be a funny aching twist in his head and he would be back in the carny days. He'd missed the afternoon performance. Big Mike would be sore. He had to get out of here and get back to the lot.

He lay and listened to his heart booming. A heavy, frightening beat. Thrum, thrum, thrum. Then there would be a subtle change of rhythm. Ta-thum, ta-thum, ta-thum.

His mind dipped and sped back to here and now. The carny was years ago. Why had George sent him here? No, it wasn't George. The cops had George. Unless that guy was bluffing, they had him good. Nailed. Along with the rest of the mob. That bitch Diana had been the cause of this. He created her image in his mind, the sneering mouth and the contemptuous eyes. Figued she was too good for

Christy, did she? He'd show her. He'd do a good job of showing her. He grinned as he remembered how she'd fallen when he'd hit her. He'd waited a long, long time for Diana. Patient waiting. And there she was, just thirty feet away. The great ropy fibrous muscles tightened and his breath came short and fast.

Then Diana turned and he saw that it was the other woman, the one who had lain under the whip of the afternoon sun.

He held his breath as she started directly toward him. She walked uncertainly. She had filled the empty bottle in the fountain and she paused to pick flowers and shove them clumsily into the neck of the bottle. She talked to herself.

Christy tried to make himself smaller. Now she stood close to him, so close that he could have reached out under the bush and touched her bare foot. It was a soiled bare foot.

When she gasped and jumped back, Christy lunged up through the brush, clamped his hand on her throat and pulled her back down to the dark place where he had been hiding. She fell like a fat sawdust doll.

He whispered, "Now when I leggo your throat, I don't want no screaming."

He took his hand away. Even in the dusk and the shadows he could see that her throat had a funny smashed look. Her face was slowly blackening, the eyes protruding, the swelling tongue growing between the lips.

One hand slapped the ground weakly and her bare heels hammered the dark damp soil at the base of a bush. She lay still. It took him quite a while to realize that she was dead. Something funny had happened to her throat.

"Diana!" he said. He shook her. "Diana!"

But it wasn't Diana, of course. He rolled his big head from side to side like a wounded bear. He crouched over her until it was full night. Then he crawled over her. As his knee with his weight on it came down on her she made a gobbling sound in her throat.

"Shut up, you," he said. He crawled on his hands and knees to the fountain. He lay on his face and put his mouth

into the water and drank deeply, as an animal drinks. Then
he stood up. His right shoulder was a great pulsating fire.
The fingers of his right hand felt swollen and stiff.

"Infection," he said aloud. He frowned and tried to
puzzle it out. Then, like a blow across the mouth, came the
vision of the suppurating leg of the boy the doctor had been
working on.

"Didn't wash his hands," Christy mumbled. "Didn't wash
his damn dirty hands. Did it on purpose."

He went to the gate and broke it open again. As he pulled
it shut behind him, he had another one of those moments
when he couldn't remember what city this was, what year
it was, where he was supposed to go. He leaned against
the wall and let the warm breeze blow against his face.
He shuddered.

Then he remembered that he had to get a car. He went
toward the *zocolo* in a lurching, ungainly walk. The *zocolo*
was brightly lighted. He pulled back into the shadows as
he saw the policeman standing sixty feet away.

A small boy tugged at his pants leg. "Geeve me money,
meester. Geeve me money, meester."

Christy slapped at him and missed. The child danced off
into the darkness, screaming at him in Spanish. The policeman turned and looked toward the mouth of the dark street.

Christy turned and ran heavily back down the street.
The breath whistled in his throat, his mouth was open as
he strained for air. The child danced along behind him,
chanting, "Geeve me money, geeve money, geeve money."

After two blocks the street was no longer paved. He
could see the flame flicker inside the open shacks of the
poor. Other children had joined the first one. They followed him, making a game of it, making a song of it. Then
there was no street and dogs snapped at his heels. He
tripped, fell, rolled among the filth and excited yammerings
of chickens. People watched him from the doorways.

The group of dogs and children grew. This was as much
fun as a fiesta. Look at the big burro! Down he goes again!
Now up again and running. Come on, *amigos!* Faster!
Geeve money, Joe. Hey, Joe! Geeve money. *Ai,* he's down

again, this time among the *puercos* of the Señora Cordoba
y Martinez. Run, *amigos*. *Ai*, hear the screams of the
señora! He runs for the *rio*.

Each breath Christy took was a sob. His side was one
vast pain and his legs were leaden. Suddenly there was a
steep pitch of bank. He saw the evil shine of the water and,
too late, tried to stop. He rolled heavily, helplessly down
the bank and into the water. It was inches deep. He stood
up, dripping wet, and saw the line of screaming, pointing
children at the crest of the bank, outlined against the last
thin light of the night sky. Dogs leaned over the edge of
the bank and barked boldly.

The shock of the water had cleared his head. Christy
looked downriver and saw the lighted bridge. He turned
and plodded out into the river. The yells of the children
grew fainter. The water came up to his knees. Walking
became more difficult. Then it was midway up his thighs.
The river seemed impossibly wide. It reached his waist,
and for the first time he felt the gentle tug of the current.

Ahead, suspended in the air, a blue neon sign high over
the town clicked on, brilliant against the blackness. The
Sage House.

With his eyes fixed on the sign, he moved steadily forward.

Tomkinton sat behind the desk of the hotel manager. Lane
Sanson sat in a chair planted squarely in front of the desk.
A ranger stood behind Lane's chair.

"Look," said Lane, "I just want to—"

"Please shut up," Tomkinton said emotionlessly.
"You've told your story. We've made arrangements to have
your 'character' witness brought over, if they can find her.
In the meantime there's nothing you can say."

"You can't treat me like a criminal."

Tomkinton smiled without humor. "We're not, so far.
We're treating you like what you are. A fool. You're one
of those people who think they can apply their own set of
special moral standards to the world. Last night a man was

killed in this town. This morning a ranger was killed and my co-worker badly injured. We're in no mood to play patty-cakes with the likes of you, Sanson. You're just a damn dilettante with so little sense you got mixed up in this mess."

"Where's Miss Saybree?"

"She's under guard. You can't see her. We have plans for her."

"She came in of her own free will, remember."

"That's something for the court to take into consideration, Sanson. We're going to clear you if we can just so we can get you out of the way. And if we can't clear you, we're going to see that you pay the maximum penalty the law allows. So don't waste your breath and my patience trying to tell us our business."

"I only—"

"For heaven's sake, shut up, can't you?"

Sanson looked down at his knuckles. He flushed. What this Tomkinton person had said was unfortunately true. He had been the worst sort of fool. The ranger behind Sanson stirred restlessly.

The door burst open and Felicia was pushed into the room. Her face was sullen and angry. She turned and tried to spit at the khaki-clad Mexican official who had pushed her. He slapped her effortlessly and turned her around so that she faced Tomkinton.

She saw Lane at once. She ran to him and took his hand in both of hers and lifted it to her lips. Her eyes danced. "Lane! I see you again. I think never."

"Get her away from him, Stan," Tomkinton said to the ranger. "You handle it."

The ranger pulled Felicia away gently. He questioned her in Spanish so fluent that Lane couldn't follow it. She nodded energetically and answered in kind, pointing first to Lane and then to herself. He could almost follow what she was saying by her gestures. As she spoke she turned often and smiled at him.

At last the ranger held up both hands to stop the flow of words. He turned to Tomkinton. "It checks out. He got

busted in the head because some of the boys working on
the case over there mistook him for Charlie Denton and
got overenthusiastic. This babe took care of him. Denton
killed one of their plainclothes cops with a knife and made
a visit to this girl's shack. There he made certain Sanson
understood that unless he brought his car across the bridge,
he could be framed for the killing of the cop. The girl says
Sanson had to leave his car at a certain garage. Just about
the time Sanson was leaving to cross the bridge they got
Charlie, as we know. I can see how this fella wouldn't want
to take a chance on trying to cross Denton."

Felicia gave out with another long spate of Spanish. The
ranger nodded. "She says that neither she nor Sanson knew
what was in the package the men wanted. She says that
Sanson is a good and honest man, but not very bright."
He grinned.

"Have her sit down over there and keep her mouth
shut," Tomkinton said. "It looks, Sanson, as though you
might turn out to be lucky, after all. Now get the Saybree
woman down here and we'll check her end of it again.
Then you can take statements from Sanson and we can
let him go."

Lane turned and smiled back over his shoulder at
Felicia. *"Muchas gracias,"* he said.

"Shut up, mister," the ranger said mildly.

Christy wasn't burning and sweating any more. Now he
had a chill so intense that he had to clamp his jaws tightly
together to keep his teeth from chattering. When he had
swum the narrow channel in the river the cool water had
soothed the fire in his shoulder. But now he had the idea
that it hadn't done him any good.

He moved through the narrow stinking alleys, guided
always by the blue letters in the sky which said "THE SAGE
HOUSE." He had lost the gun in the river, or else while
he was running from the children. He couldn't remember.

The river had washed away much of the filth, but his
clothes still had a fetid odor. The swelling had spread down

to his hand. It was visibly larger than his left hand and was a darker color.

He waited in doorways to avoid being seen. He was finding it hard to remember why he had to get to the hotel. It was all tangled in his mind. The girl was there, with the money. Shaymen had let him down. Then it seemed that he'd killed the girl back there near a fountain. It made his head hurt to try to straighten it all out. The only thing he was absolutely certain of was the great need to get to the hotel. When he reached the hotel he would remember why it was important.

And he wondered if he would ever be warm again.

It took time and planning to cross the main street. He had to go four blocks from the hotel and then wait a long time before he knew it was safe. Once he sat down in a doorway and before he knew it his eyes had closed. He awakened when he fell out of the doorway, his cheek against cinders.

Again there was the network of alleys and small streets. At last he came out into an open place which he recognized as the parking lot behind the hotel. He could not risk the alley entrance to the parking lot. There was too much danger of a car coming in or going out, fixing him in its lights. The other wall of the hotel was separated from the wall of a store by a space so narrow that he had to turn his shoulders to get into it.

He sidestepped along. Soon there was a lighted window above his head. He jumped up and grabbed the sill. With effortless strength, he pulled his heavy body up to where he could look in. It was the dining room. He clung there, looking at the people at the tables. He knew none of them. He tried to remember why he had come back here. Puzzled, he dropped back and continued his slow movement.

The next window was dark. The one after that was lighted. It was a bit higher than the last one. He missed the sill on the first jump.

On the second jump his fingers locked on the sill. He wondered vaguely why his right shoulder was so sore. He chinned himself on the sill and looked in.

It was a small room. An office. He saw her at once. Diana. Now he knew that she wasn't dead. But her face had a funny, dead look about it. The window was open from the top but he couldn't hear what she was saying to the young round-faced man behind the desk because of the funny roaring sound in his ears.

And that man sitting beside her. Now it was becoming clearer. Diana and that man. He remembered the man throwing something at him. A great blow against his head. There was a ranger, a Mexican girl and a Mexican official of some kind in the room. Christy gave them one quick glance. He wasn't interested in them.

He dropped back to the ground to give himself time to think. George stood beside him, smiling his funny crooked smile.

"What the hell are you doing here, George?" he whispered.

George's voice came from far away. It had a hollow sound. "I thought you might forget what I told you to do, Christy. I hear you've been crossing me up."

"I wouldn't do a thing like that, George. Honest!"

"You got to get in there and kill both of them, Christy. Diana and that friend of hers. You can do that."

"There's a couple of cops in there, George," he complained.

"Remember, Christy, how strong you are. You can do it. If you don't do it, I'll know for sure you're crossing me, Christy."

"I'll try, George. I'll sure try. You know me."

He glanced down the narrow space between the buildings to make sure no one was watching. When he looked back, George was gone. He blinked a few times and decided that George didn't want to hang around. Or maybe he just couldn't see him. It was hard to see since he'd lost his glasses. He wondered where he'd left them.

Too bad about the gun. With the gun, he could hang up there on the sill and pot both of them. Now he would have to do it another way. He moved to the side of the window and put his back against the store wall, his feet against the hotel wall. He began to hitch his way up. It was slow work. Finally he was on a level with the window. Then, maintaining the pressure, he hitched sideways until at last his feet, spread wide, were on the sill. He straightened his legs and his shoulders slid up the store wall. He flattened his hands against the wall and shoved himself toward the window as hard as he could, ducking his head below the upper sill. He hit the center bar of the sash, carrying screen, sash, glass and all forward with him into the room. He landed lightly on the balls of his feet, pawing at the ranger with what looked like a foolishly light blow. Yet it dropped the man over into the corner beside the desk.

As Diana jumped up he grabbed her with one big arm. With his raised foot he shoved hard against the front of the desk. The desk slammed Tomkinton brutally against the wall.

Laughing aloud, Christy held the kicking, struggling girl in one arm. His left hand caught Sanson by the throat as Sanson tried to come up out of the chair where he had been frozen with shock.

Then, as Christy yelled for George to come see what he was doing, a pain like a flame seared across the backs of his legs just above the knees. The strength went out of his legs and he fell heavily. He saw Diana roll free and scramble over to where Sanson stood, turning in his arms to look at Christy on the floor.

Christy leaned his head back and looked up into the broad-boned smiling face of the Mexican girl. Her dark eyes glittered like the onyx that had once been carved into knives for the use of the priests of the sun god. She showed her even white teeth as she smiled down at him.

The red-bladed knife gleamed in her hand.

From an enormous distance he heard the ranger saying in a dazed voice, "By God, she hamstrung him! She had that knife taped to her thigh and she come up behind him crouched as though she were going to cut the grass, and she hamstrung him!"

The wave of darkness hung above him, a silent dark crest, and then it fell forward onto him, spinning him down into it.

10

THE LETTERS HAD COME TO HIS DESK IN THE newsroom in Houston. The first two weeks had been difficult, but now he knew that he'd be able to hold his own. The first big story he had brought them, an eye-witness account of all that trouble down at Baker, had helped. They'd slapped a by-line on it, too.

The first letter was from his agent. Dear Lane,

It is nice to have you rise from the dead and have you say in your letter that you're going to keep on working. From the last mss, I'd say you need a lot of work. *A Daughter of Many Kings* has its moments, but it suffers from a lack of discipline and plan. Work from your carbon and see if you can send me a tighter version. And shorter. This novella form is an awkward length for that sort of thing.

He grinned and put the letter in his desk drawer, then opened the other one.

Lane dear,

I suppose you follow the news and I suppose it is no news to you that I'm going to be a sort of house guest for a year and a day. My lawyer says I'm very lucky, and I guess I can live through it. I am writing this while waiting for the transportation to my new address. George drew twenty and it doesn't seem half long enough, somehow. Vindictive sort, aren't I?

Anyway, Lane, I wanted you to know that you straightened me out when I needed it and I'm grateful. A year and a day from now I will have decided what sort of new life I want. It will be a law-abiding and uneventful one, believe me. I hope some day to do you a favor in return—if I haven't *already* done it.

                                        Your
                                        Diana

He shrugged. The last part of the letter seemed incoherent. Not hard to understand how a girl in her spot might be a little incoherent.

He put her letter in the drawer, too, stood up and clapped his hat on the back of his head. The managing editor came across the newsroom toward him.

"How's it going, Lane?"

"Good, thanks."

"Say, you'll have no trial to cover down the line. The infection finally killed that Christy citizen. They didn't get the arm off soon enough, I guess."

Lane sighed. "That suits me."

"By the way, that was a nice job you did on the transit squabble."

"Thanks again."

He left, whistling. He went down the stairs, grinned in at the girls behind the classified ad counter.

As he reached the outside door he saw, out of the corner of his eye, a girl coming quickly toward him. He turned and gasped. "Sandy! Sandy, what—"

Her eyes were shining. "Don't talk, darling. Just walk with me."

Her hand was through his arm as they walked down the sidewalk. He smiled down into her face and she squeezed his arm lightly.

"I had to shut you up, you oaf," she said. "I was about to cry."

"I remember that you cry nicely. Sandy, why did you come here?"

"To see my ex," she said smugly.

He stopped and faced her. "I'm no good for you. Didn't we find that out?"

"Hush. I might give you a second chance. If you want it."

"If I want it!"

"I'll think it over, oaf."

"After what I did to you, Sandy?"

"Or what I did to you. Damn a wife who runs out when she's worst needed."

"I chased you out."

"You did *not*. I left."

"By special request. Who cares? You're back. But how come? How did it happen?"

She took his arm again. "Come on, keep walking. You see, I got a letter. From a girl. Quite a girl, I think. She mentioned that she ran into you and you seemed to be carrying a torch for one gal named Sandy, so she wormed the address out of you. It was signed Diana Saybree."

"So that's what she meant!" he said.

"What, darling?"

"Never mind. Look, I've got a small apartment just three blocks from here. There's ice, gin and vermouth. They need a woman's touch."

He quickened his pace but she stopped and made her eyes wide. "But I can't! I just remembered."

"What? A date?"

"No, I just remembered that I'm a single woman. Heavens! I'd be compromised."

"Huh!" he said.

She laughed in the old well-remembered way. Again she took his arm. "Come on, you big mental hazard. What's your address?"

Linda

LOOKING BACK, I THINK IT WAS RIGHT AFTER the first of the year that Linda started hammering at me to take my vacation in the fall intsead of in the summer. Hammering isn't exactly the word. That wasn't Linda's way. She started by talking about Stu and Betty Carbonelli and what a fine time they'd had when they went south for their vacation in November. And she talked about the terrible traffic in the summer and how dangerous it was. And about how not having kids made it easier too.

I kept my head down, thinking that this would blow over like most of her ideas. I wasn't at all keen on this one. I knew it would mean more expense. Linda never thought or talked about money except when we didn't have enough for something she wanted to do or wanted to buy, and then she had plenty to say. Actually, I never cared much for vacations. Sure, I like to get away from the plant for a while, but I'm content to stay around the house. I've got my woodworking tools in the cellar, and I like to fool around in the yard. There's plenty to do.

Three years ago we did stay right at home. I thought it was the best vacation we ever had, but Linda kept saying it was the worst. This was the first year I was due to get three weeks with pay instead of just two, and she brought that up too, telling me how it would give us a real chance to get away.

I hoped it would blow over and I'd be able to talk her into taking the last three weeks in August. In fact, I put in for that early, in March. I thought we could rent a camp up at Lake Pleasant. That would mean only a seventy-mile trip and a chance for some fishing.

But Linda kept harping on it. Now, of course, I know why she kept after me the way she did. I know the horror that lived in the back of her mind all those months she was cooing and wheedling. Now that it's too late, I can look back and see just how carefully it was all arranged.

Ever since Christmas we had been seeing quite a lot of the Jeffries. His first name was Brandon, but nobody would ever call him that. You instinctively called him Jeff. They were a little younger than Linda and me, and he was with the same company, but on the sales end, while I've been in the purchasing department for the past nine years —in fact ever since I got out of the army and married Linda. Jeff was one of the top salesmen on the road and last year they brought him in and made him sales manager of the northeastern division. He got an override on all the sales made in his division and had to make only about three trips a month. I guess he made out pretty well— probably a lot better than I do—and on top of that Stella, his wife, had some money of her own.

When they brought him in last year Jeff and Stella bought two adjoining lots about a block and a half from our place and put up quite a house. A little more modern than I go for, but Linda was just crazy about it. Linda always seemed to take a big shine to people who had more to do with than we did, and so it was always a strain trying to keep up. I tried to save a little, but it was a pretty slow process.

The four of us played bridge and canasta pretty often. Usually I don't like to see too much of people who work at the same place because it's like bringing your work home with you. But Jeff was in an entirely different division and we didn't talk about the company at all.

Daytimes, Linda would go over and gab with Stella, or vice versa. They didn't ever seem to become real good friends, if you know what I mean. We saw a lot of each other, but there was always a little reserve. Nobody ever seemed to let their hair down all the way. Maybe some of that was my fault. I have about two or three close friends, and a lot of people I just happen to know. I've always been quiet. Linda did the talking for both of us.

If you've ever been in purchasing, where you have to see the salesmen, you'll know what I mean when I say that Jeff was a perfect salesman type. Not the cartoon type, slapping backs and breathing in your face, but the modern type of top sales hand—tall and good-looking in a sort of rugged way. When he told jokes, they were on himself. He'd listen when you talked. I mean really listen, drawing you out. He had that knack of making you feel important. I'm sure he wasn't really interested in my wood-working shop, but he'd come down to the cellar and pretend to be. I probably bored him, showing him how the stuff worked, but you'd never guess it.

Jeff kept himself in shape too. He really worked at it— swimming and tennis and so on. And I guess he had a sun lamp home because he had a good tan the year round. All of which added to the kind of impression he made.

When you're married to a woman like Linda, you develop a sort of sixth sense for those jokers who are on the make. We couldn't ever go to a big party without somebody trying to hang all over her. I hate parties like that, but they made Linda sparkle. She was thirty-four when we met the Jeffries and looked about twenty-six or seven. People were all the time telling her that she looked like Paulette Goddard, but I never could see it.

One thing Linda really had, and that's a beautiful figure. I have never seen a better figure anywhere, on anybody. She had to watch her weight pretty carefully. She liked to stay at a hundred and twenty-five. Personally, I liked her at about a hundred and thirty-two, because when she weighed less her face looked sort of gaunt.

But like I was saying, you develop a sixth sense when you have a wife like Linda. I watched Jeff pretty closely, worrying a little bit, because if anybody had a chance of making out, that Jeff Jeffries certainly would. But I could see that it was all right. They kidded around a lot, with him making a burlesque pass at her now and then, but I could see it was all in fun. And he was very loving with

Stella, his wife, holding her hand whenever he could, and
kissing her on the temple when they danced together at
the club and that sort of thing. Which is funny when you
think of it, because Stella Jeffries certainly was anything
but a good-looking woman. She was just awfully nice.
Really nice. I liked her a lot, more than I liked Jeff.

It certainly surprised me that I ever got to marry Linda
Willestone. That was her name in high school, when I
first knew her. We were in the same graduating class. She
claimed that she remembered me, but I don't think she
really did. It was a big school, about seven thousand total
enrollment, and I was even quieter then than I am now. I
worked after school most of the time, so I didn't have a
chance to get in on those extra things a lot of the others
did. Linda belonged to a different world. She was in just
one of my classes. I was shy then. I thought about her a
lot, at night, but it would have been just as easy for me
to chop off my right hand as go up and say anything to
her in the hall between classes. She ran around with a
gang that included all the big shots in the student body.
I didn't see her again after I graduated, but I used to think
about her from time to time and wonder what happened
to her.

I got out of the army and got a job and a week later I
saw her on the street and recognized her. I walked right
up to her and said, "Hello, Linda." She looked at me
blankly. I told her who I was and how I'd been in high
school with her. We went into a place and had coffee.
Then I saw that she didn't look good at all. She looked
as if she'd been sick. Her clothing was shabby. All the
life she had had in high school seemed to have faded.

She said frankly that she was broke and looking for a
job. She'd come in on a bus from California. It was a
pretty tragic story she told me. Her people were dead. She
had married a marine and he'd been killed. He hadn't
transferred his insurance to her and his people, Kentucky
people, wouldn't have anything to do with her because

the marine had married her instead of a girl in his home town.

She had worked for a while in California and then married an Air Force warrant officer. He got in some kind of a jam and had been given a dishonorable discharge and it was after that happened that she found out he'd already had a wife and two children back in Caribou, Maine. She'd worked some more and gotten sick and when sickness took her savings, she'd been a charity patient until she was well enough to leave. She'd worked just long enough to get together the bus fare to come home.

They talked about the war being rough on men, but I guess you could say that Linda was just as much a war casualty as any man. What happened to her had just taken the heart out of her, and it made me feel bad to see the way she was. I guess what I did was pick her up and dust her off and put the heart back in her. You could call it a rebound on her part, I guess. Not a rebound from any specific man, but a rebound from life. For me it was fine, because I never thought I would get to marry Linda Willestone. I could still remember the times in high school when I would be leaving to walk to my after-school job, and I'd see Linda hurrying out to get into a car with a whole bunch of kids and go driving off somewhere, laughing and having a good time.

They always say that the first year of marriage is the hardest. With us I think it was the best. At first Linda seemed tired all the way through, but as the months went by she began to come alive more and more. She was fond of me and grateful to me. I did not demand that she love me. I hoped it would come later, but when it didn't seem to, I didn't mind too much. It was enough to have her around, and know that wherever we went, people looked at her.

It's hard for a man to assess his own marriage. He cannot say if it is good or bad. Maybe no marriage is entirely good or bad. I know only that after that first year there was strain between us. Linda wanted a life that I didn't

want. I told her her values were superficial; she told me
life was more than waiting for death. There were no blaz-
ing quarrels. My temper is not of that breed. And in the
last few years things became easier between us. We worked
out a sort of compromise. She lived my way, and when
we could afford it, she would take a trip, usually to
Chicago. That seemed to ease her nervous tension.

I had hoped, of course, that we would have children.
But that was denied us. The doctor she went to said that
it had something to do with how sick she had been in
California. It would have done much to end her restlessness, I thought, but since it could not be, we managed to
work out a life with a minimum of strain. Sometimes, out
of irritation, she would say cruel things to me, calling me a
nonentity, a zero, a statistic. But I understood, or I thought
I did. She was an earthy, hot-blooded woman, and our life
was pretty quiet. I understand a great deal more about her
now.

During the past year she began to take an almost frantic
interest in her appearance, spending a lot of money on
creams and lotions, taking strange diets, working hard on
grotesque exercises that claimed to firm up this part or
that, remove slack or wrinkles here and there. That too,
in the light of what happened, becomes significant.

To round out this picture of Linda, I must add in all
fairness that she was a superb housekeeper. I believe that
was the result of her energy and restlessness. The house
always gleamed. Though the food she cooked was plain
and unimaginative, she always prepared it quickly, with a
minimum of fuss and effort, and did her marketing with
the relentless efficiency that made me jokingly offer to
hire her in the purchasing department at the plant. She
was good with her clothes too. Though she spent an uncomfortable amount, her wardrobe was much larger than
even that amount would justify. The one project I completed in my cellar shop that pleased her the most was a
special closet for her wardrobe. I walled off one end of
her bedroom with mirrored doors in such a way that the
doors could be completely folded out of the way, or so

arranged that she could stand and get a multiple view of herself. I built in overhead cupboards for her hats, designed a long shoe rack, built in one set of wide shallow drawers that reached from the floor to shoulder height. It took me over two months of my spare time. Hanging the doors so they would roll easily was the trickiest part. Sometimes on rainy Sundays she would shut herself in her room and try on practically everything she owned, putting a lot of things aside for changes and alterations during the week.

As I said, I had already put in for a summer vacation and didn't tell Linda, because I was waiting for this idea of a fall vacation to blow over. One night in late March or early April Jeff and Stella had come over. It was when we'd finished a rubber of bridge and were talking while I made fresh drinks that Linda told them about her idea, and how Stu and Betty Carbonelli had had such a good time.

"Betty said that you can get beach cottages for practically nothing on the west coast of Florida in October and November because their season doesn't really start down there until around Christmas. They were on Verano Key, quite a way south of Sarasota. They said they had the whole beach to themselves."

As I put the filled glasses down on the bridgetable, Jeff said, "You know, that sounds pretty good to me. What do you think, Stell?"

"I've never been on the west coast. When I was little we used to go down to Palm Beach a lot. Sis still has a big place there, but it's rented every year through an agent. She never liked it."

The bridge game was ignored while we all talked it over. I said it was too far to go for just three weeks, particularly if, as Stu Carbonelli said, you had to have a car. You could subtract six days for the trip, going and coming. A full week gone out of three.

Jeff thought that over for quite a while, frowning, and then he interrupted Stella and said, "Hey! Here's a deal. We have to have a car, right? We could rent places close together. I could fix it, Paul, so that my three weeks would start four days after yours. You and Linda could drive down and Stell and I could fly down. Then when your time was up, you both could fly back and Stell and I could leave at the same time and drive back. If we were close together, we would only need one car, wouldn't we? And then we'd both have two weeks and four days down there. Driving both ways is a chore. But just one way . . ."

"And we could put all the heavy luggage for both of us in the car, so it wouldn't mean messing with a lot of baggage on the plane trip," Linda said eagerly.

Actually, Jeff's idea made it sound a lot better. I didn't want to take our vacation along with the Jeffries if we were going to be in an expensive place, because I knew we couldn't keep up with them. But Stu had talked a lot about the place they had gone, and it certainly wasn't any Miami. He said that the nearest town, Hooker, was eight miles from the key, and to get off the key you drive over a rattly old one-lane wooden bridge. He had said there was quite a bit of commercial fishing in the area. He had said you could eat, sleep, fish and swim, and aside from that, if you wanted any night life of any special splendor, you had to go to Miami or Havana. If the Jeffries wanted to make a side trip, there was no reason why we had to go along with them. And Stu had raved about plug casting for snook by moonlight in Little Hurricane Pass at the south end of Verano Key.

Stella, who had been dubious at first, gradually became enthusiastic, and the three of them concentrated their forces on me. I brought up every objection I could think of, and every time one of them would answer it.

Like I said, I'm quiet. And I'm pretty stubborn too. I guess those things go together pretty often. There they were, the three of them all heckling me. Florida had begun to sound better to me, but it was the idea of the three of them leaning on me that put my back up. I finally said flatly that I'd decided to take my vacation in August and go up to Lake Pleasant. It certainly dampened that party right down. Maybe I sounded cross when I said it.

I was sorry to see Jeff and Stella leave so early, because I knew Linda would be gunning for me. This would be one of the big screaming brawls she could throw every so often, yapping at me in a shrill way that would make me dizzy.

But it didn't work out that way at all. She was quiet after Jeff and Stella left. I helped clean up the place, waiting every minute for the explosion. It just didn't come. We went on up to bed.

Right here, in order to tell how that night was, I guess I've got to explain a little about the physical side of our marriage.

I'd never been with a woman until we were married. I kind of resented her knowing more about it than I did, but in some ways I was glad she did because it made things a lot easier at first. She was always moody about it. By that I mean that sometimes she'd seem to want to and a lot of the time she wouldn't. It was generally pretty quick the times she'd want to, and the times she didn't she acted like she was bored and just wished it would be over.

Anyway, on this night after Jeff and Stella went home and we went up to bed with me waiting for the explosion, it didn't come. She fooled around and I was in bed first. Finally, she came out of the bathroom and stood in the doorway with the light from the bathroom shining right through some sort of filmy thing I'd never seen on her before. I guessed later that she'd bought it for the trip to Florida, after I knew why she bought it.

She stood there for a long time. As I said, I've never seen a better figure on a woman in my life. She turned the light off, finally, and I could hear the rustling of her as she came toward me in the darkness, hear the rustling, and then smell a new kind of heavy perfume she had put on, and then feel her strong arms around me as she brought her lips down on mine there in our dark bedroom.

When it was all over, she lay in my arms and she said, "This is the way it should always be, darling. Now you know why I want us to go to Florida. I want a new start for our marriage. I want a second honeymoon, a proper honeymoon this time."

Well, I knew I wanted it to happen again just that way, and if I had to go to Florida to guarantee it, then I would go to Florida. It was as though I hadn't even been married before. She was like a stranger, and I fell in love with her all over again.

In the morning she called Stella Jeffries. I told Jeff down at the plant. And it was all set.

Rufus Stick, the director of purchasing, tried to dissuade me. He said that the fall was a bad time to leave. But when he saw that I really wanted that time, he went along with it. We both knew that he owed me a lot. I devised the new spot check control of our perpetual inventory system and installed it. It works like a charm. And I set up the statistical control of inspection of incoming materials and revamped our point-of-reorder control system so that production hasn't been on our necks in over a year. Besides, Rufus Stick knew that I didn't want his job. I couldn't handle the contacts with the top brass of other sections. I also owed Rufus a lot. He let me do my work in my own way, and raised me when he could. It was a good working relationship. He knew he had a loyal man under him who knew his job, and I knew that Rufus would protect me in every way he could.

We settled on Friday, October 22, as my final working day and I would report back on Monday, November 15. As soon as that was arranged. I phoned Jeff from my office and he said he would get to work on it. He phoned me that evening at home and said he'd gotten approval to start his vacation on Wednesday, October 27, and he would have to be back at work on Thursday, November 17. It gave him only twenty-two days to my twenty-three, but that was because of starting in the middle of the week.

I guess that he didn't have much trouble arranging it because, from what I could hear, he was the fair-haired boy in sales. They were using him more and more on contacts with the advertising agency in addition to his regular job, and the new campaign he had worked on was turning

out to be very successful. Contact work like that demands
a talent I just don't have. I find it very hard to talk to
strangers. Once when I was in grammar school I tried to
sell soap from door to door in my own neighborhood. I
would press my finger against the door frame beside the
bell rather than press the bell.

It was about a week after that when Linda had the
Jeffries and the Carbonellis over one night. Stu brought
his 35 millimeter slides and a portable projector and we
took down a picture so Stu could flash the slides on the
wall. Stu kept moaning because he had to take his vacation in July this year, and kept telling us how he envied us.
The slides were fine. He gave me a lot of information on
the fishing and said he'd even bring some good snook plugs
to the office and leave them with me. Betty gave the girls
the pitch on the marketing and so on. They gave us the
name of the man who owned the beach cottages and rented
them himself. Jeff said he would write on a company
letterhead and make the arrangements. The man's name
was Dooley. Stu said he was a retired construction worker
who had built the two beach cottages himself. Stu said
the only bad thing about their vacation had been that during the last week of it the other cottage had been rented
to some South Carolina people with four noisy children,
but if we wrote early enough and sewed up both cottages,
we could avoid that.

Stu and Betty had to leave early because of their sitter.
We sat around and talked about the pictures and what we
would take. We had a mild argument about which car we
would take. It was mild because I certainly didn't want to
subject Jeff and Stella to driving back in our six-year-old
sedan, not after the cars he was used to driving. Jeff was
perceptive about it. He said, "Look, kids, I've got a new
one on order for delivery next month. By October it will
be nicely broken in, and there'll be plenty of room in it
for all our junk." So we left it at that.

Jeff heard from Dooley ten days later, saying that we
could rent both cottages for the full month of November,
and he would let us take occupancy the last week in Oc-

tober. He wanted a hundred and fifty apiece for the cottages, plus four fifty for the Florida tax. It was twenty-five more than Stu and Betty had paid, but still reasonable. I gave Jeff my check for my share, and he mailed the full rental to Dooley. Dooley wrote back and said he would be away when we arrived, but we could pick up the keys to both places at Jethro's Market in Hooker, and he said that before he left he'd make certain that everything was shipshape at the two cottages. He said he hoped we'd have a good vacation, and if there was any trouble about anything, any repairs to be made, we should please see Lottie Jethro at the market.

We had one of the hottest, stickiest summers on record. Even the baking city couldn't subdue Linda's enthusiasm for the trip. It seemed to mean an awful lot to her. It puzzled me a bit. I could understand how she could reach such a peak of enthusiasm if we were going to Paris or Rome or something, but she was brittle and nervous and quick, as though she expected the sandy expanses of Verano Key to contain the glamor and excitement of a royal court. I can see now how, in a special sense, that is what Linda went there to find.

Jeff's car came and I drove it a couple of times that summer when the four of us went out together. It was low, long, pale gray and powerful. It had power brakes, power steering, power seats, power windows and startling acceleration. It rode so smoothly that it would be up to seventy before you were aware that you were speeding. When I went back to my own car after driving that monster I had the feeling that I was sitting nine feet off the ground and all the fenders were chattering. I must say that I looked forward to driving that thing all the way to Florida.

Actually, we did not see as much of the Jeffries that summer as I had thought we would. They belonged to the country club and we didn't. On the hot days Jeff would go right to the club from the office, and Stella would be there by the pool waiting for him. I expected Linda to start her annual campaign to get me to join, but she didn't. She was very easy to get along with that summer. She sang when she worked. She took sunbaths in our small back yard. I had made a frame for her and tacked striped canvas on it so she could have privacy. She sunbathed in the nude, oiling herself heavily so as not to harshen her skin, until she was the same even golden tan from head to toe.

I remembered one Saturday when I was working in the yard and she was in the small canvas pen sunbathing. I walked over and my footsteps were soundless on the grass. She lay on her back with little joined white plastic cups over her eyes. They made her face look most odd. I thought she was asleep, and then I saw that she had a cigarette between her fingers. She brought it slowly to her lips, inhaled, held the smoke in her lungs and then slowly blew it out. I wondered what she was thinking about. The plastic shielding over her eyes gave her such a secretive look. Sweat stood in tiny droplets on her brown skin. Her body was of such perfection, there under the sun, that it wasn't like looking at a nude living woman. It was strangely like looking at statuary, at something very ancient and very perfect—something brought forward to this era out of a crueler past.

I had the odd feeling that I did not know her at all. It was much like the times in high school when I had stared, flushing, at the curve of her young breast, unable to look away, caught not by lust but by mystery. And throughout my nighttime imaginings of her during those young years I had thought deeply and forlornly that this special mystery would never be for me—that I would never content myself with lesser flesh and thus would go through life tragically alone.

I spoke her name and she removed the white plastic cups and squinted up at me and said, "What? What is it?"

She was Linda again and I went back to my yard work. I know now what she was thinking as I stood watching her, and I have come to believe that evil radiates its own special aura so that when you are receptive to it, you can feel a brush of coldness across your heart.

But that day I shrugged it off, not recognizing it for what it was. I was merely Paul Cowley, a mild man who grubbed away at the crab grass—a man of average height with a narrow introspective face, sloping shoulders, no-color hair that in the past year had thinned so much on top that under the fluorescent bathroom light I could see the gleam of my scalp under the sparse hair. I knew what I was. I was a worker, with a dogged analytical mind, and hands that were clever with both tools and figures. I had outgrown my boyhood dreams of triumph. I knew my place in my known world, with my work and my home and my restless and beautiful wife.

I now know that that Paul Cowley was a fool, and it is of such fools that you read in your tabloids. They believe they walk forward on a wide safe place, whereas in truth it is an incredibly narrow walkway, high over blackness.

THE HEAT CONTINUED FOR TWO WEEKS AFTER Labor Day. It turned cool then and the leaves began to change. I put my fishing tackle in order, bought traveler's checks, bought the sort of beach clothing I thought I would need. I worked long hours at the office, determined that my desk would be absolutely clear on the day I left. I knew there would be enough of an accumulation by the time I returned.

The last days seemed to drag. At last it was Friday, the twenty-second. I said good-by to the people in the section and said good-by to Rufus. It seemed odd to be taking off after the summer was over. I left my address with Rufus— Route 1, Box 88, Hooker, Florida—so he could contact me if necessary. He said he hoped he wouldn't have to.

On Friday evening Jeff and Stella brought the big car over. Their stuff was all packed in it, and ours was ready to load. Jeff brought our plane tickets for the trip back and I gave him a check. They would arrive at the Sarasota air-port at seven-twenty on the evening of the twenty-seventh. We should arrive at the key on the twenty-fifth, and that would give us time to get settled before running up to

Sarasota to get them. They took my car when they left, and my garage door key. They would use my car and leave it in my garage before they left.

Linda and I loaded the car and went to bed. In the morning we closed up the house, got an early start, had breakfast on the road. We arrived in Hooker on Monday evening at five o'clock. The trip was uneventful. The car drove easily. Linda was uncommonly quiet during the trip. We had no difficulty finding rooms at pleasant motels as there were not many people on the road at that time of year. We drove from the crisp bite of fall back into summer.

Hooker was a small sleepy town dotted with the crumbling Moorish palaces of the old boom of the twenties. Its streets fanned optimistically out into the palmetto scrub, tall weeds thrusting up through shattered asphalt. It was still and hot and there were a few dusty cars parked on the wide main street. I parked in front of Jethro's Market and when I got out of the car two large black lethargic mosquitoes landed on my forearm.

Lottie Jethro was a vast faded young woman, with a cotton dress stretching tightly across her abundances. She gave me the keys and said, "You go right on out this road. It runs along the bay and then you come to a sign points west says Verano Key Beach. Get out onto the key and turn left, that's south, and go about a mile and you come to a little sign says Cypress Cottages, and that's it. You'll have to try the keys because I don't know which is which. But they're both alike. The fuses on the electric is unscrewed. You got to screw them in. There's fresh bottles of gas there for both, and just the one pump house, here's the key. There's a sign on the wall telling how you prime the pump."

The screen door banged and Linda came in after me. She had changed to shorts for the last day's travel. Some men in the back of the store stopped talking when she came in.

"I thought we might as well pick up some groceries now," she said.

"We got a good line of frozen meats and groceries, lady," Miss Jethro said.

I bought cigarettes and some magazines and some insect spray and repellent and looked over the fishing tackle while Linda completed her purchasing. I had to cash a traveler's check to pay for everything. We drove about six miles south and found the sign and crossed a frail wooden bridge onto the key. The road down the key was a sand road, the hump in the middle so high that it brushed the differential. We passed two houses that looked closed. The sun was settling toward the steel blue Gulf. Sometimes the road would wind near enough so that we could see a wide expanse of pale beach and lazy waves that heaved up and slapped at the sand. Water birds ran busily along the water line, pecking at the sand.

"Pretty nice," I said.

"Yes," Linda said.

The two cottages were about a hundred feet apart. I asked her which one she wanted and she said it didn't make any difference. I parked by the southerly one. I unlocked the door and we carried our things in. We unlocked the other one and looked it over. They were alike. The key was narrow there, and there was a long dock out into the bay at the back, and a rowboat overturned on the bank near the dock, above the high tide mark. The pump house was not far from the dock. Both cottages were of cypress, weathered gray. They each had two bedrooms, a living room with furniture upholstered in a vicious shade of green plastic, small gas heaters, gas stove, fireplace, refrigerator, tiny kitchen, a screened porch about ten by ten on the front looking across the sand road toward the Gulf.

I got the electricity going in each cottage, got the pump started, and then drove the car over to the other cottage and unloaded the Jeffries' things, trying to put them where I thought they would want them. In addition to the usual luggage, they had packed a new badminton set and a gun case. I opened the gun case to see what Jeff had thought he would use. It was a Remington bolt action .22 with a four power scope. It looked new and it looked as though it would be fun for plinking at beer cans.

Linda had the food put away by the time I got back, and had started unpacking our bags. When we were through we took a walk down the beach. The big hot red sun was just sliding into the Gulf. About four hundred yards south of us was a big house with hurricane shutters over the large windows. Almost an equal distance north of us were four small beach cabins that were deserted and badly in need of paint.

"We're certainly alone here."

She didn't answer me. With darkness came more mosquitoes. We took refuge on the porch. Linda made sandwiches. I plugged in our new portable radio and we listened to Cuban music from Havana. The waves made a soft sound on the beach. I couldn't stop yawning. I went out and moved the car around to the bay side of the cottage so there'd be less chance of salt spray damaging it. When I went to bed Linda was still listening to the music.

WHEN I GOT UP IN THE MORNING, LINDA WAS gone. I put on swimming trunks and went out on the beach. I could see her on the beach, far to the north, a tiny figure that bent over now and then to pick up shells. I was on my second cup of coffee when I heard her under the outside shower. She came into the kitchen in a few minutes wrapped in a big yellow towel, her soaked bathing suit in her hand. "That water must be eighty degrees!" she said. "And there were big things out there, sort of rolling. I'll bet they were porpoises." Her eyes were shining, and she looked like a child on Saturday.

I picked up a burn that afternoon that was still uncomfortable when we drove up to Sarasota on Wednesday to meet the plane. It was a small plane that brought them down from Tampa International. It was dark and Jeff said that I better keep right on driving because I knew the road. They said they had a fine trip down. They said it had snowed a little at home on Sunday but it had melted as

soon as it hit the ground. Jeff seemed boisterous and ex-
uberant, but I thought Stella was rather quiet. Linda spent
most of the trip back turned around in the seat telling them
about the layout. We all seemed a little strained with each
other, and I guessed it was because we were all wondering
how it was going to work out, four people taking a vacation
together. It could be fine, or it could be a mess.

Jeff was awed by the primitive condition of the key
road as shown by our headlights and by the lurching of
the big car. I drove them up to their door with a flourish,
and Linda went in first and turned the lights on for them.
She had turned on their refrigerator the previous day, and
stocked it with breakfast things.

They seemed pleased with the setup, particularly Jeff.
That surprised me a little because, as with Linda, I thought
he would be more likely to be enthusiastic about a more
civilized environment. When they were settled we went over
and sat on their porch and talked for a while. Stella said
she was sleepy but not to go yet. She went in to bed and
the three of us talked some more.

That evening was the last time that the four of us were
what I would call normal with each other. It all started
the next day. It started without warning and there didn't
seem to be anything I could do about it, or Stella could do
about it. Here is exactly the way it happened.

At about ten o'clock we were all out on the beach. We
had two blankets and towels and a faded old beach umbrella I had found in the pump house. I remember that
I had a program of dance music on the portable radio. Both
Stella and I had to be careful of the sun. Jeff had a good
tan. Linda, of course, was browner than anybody. Our
voices sounded far away and sleepy, the way they do when
the sun is hot.

Linda got up. She stood there with her shadow falling
across me. I thought she was going to go in swimming. She
said, "Come on, Jeff." I thought she was asking him to go
in with her. But her tone of voice had seemed oddly harsh.
Jeff got up without a word and the two of them walked
down the beach, headed south.

I don't think I can explain exactly why it created such an awkward situation. Certainly Linda and Jeff could walk together, as could Stella and I, should we want to. The four of us were, I thought, friends. But it was the manner in which they left us. Linda's tone had been peremptory, autocratic. Jeff had obeyed immediately. It spoke of a relationship that I had not suspected. Had it been done in a normal way, they would have said something about walking down the beach, and coming back soon, and don't get too much sun—like that. They just left.

Though you could see up the beach a long way to the north, you could not see far to the south. The big house south of us was on a sort of headland, and beyond it the beach curved inward and out of our range of vision.

Each time I looked they were further away, walking steadily. Then I looked and they were gone. Now this is also hard to explain. Their action made me revert to the way I had felt about Linda many years ago. She had walked off, out of reach. She was back with the beautiful people. I was again the Paul Cowley who worked after school and knew so few people in our class.

I could not help glancing at Stella, wondering how she was taking it. She wore heavy sun glasses with tilted frames and very dark lenses. Her eyes were hidden behind them. I thought of any number of inane things I could say, but in the end I said nothing.

After a time Stella got up without a word, took off her sunglasses and watch, tucked her pale hair into a white bathing cap and went down to the water. She swam far out with a lithe power at odds with the frail look of her body. I watched her float out there. After what seemed a long time, she swam slowly in and walked up and sat in the shade of the beach umbrella, arms hugging her knees, looking out to sea. Our silence with each other was awkward. The longer Jeff and Linda stayed away, the more awkward it became. I thought back over the relationship between Jeff and my wife. There seemed to be nothing to justify what they had done—rather, the way they had done what they had done.

A quiz program started and I turned off the portable.

"Well, Paul," Stella said quietly. She came originally, I believe, from Hartford. Her voice had that flat quality, that special accent that women who come from that area and go to exclusive finishing schools acquire.

"I . . . what do you mean?"

"You wouldn't ask if you didn't know. She could have had a sign painted, I suppose. Or branded his forehead. I don't think she could have made it any more obvious."

"I don't think it's that way."

"I don't think it's any other way. I didn't want to come here. I did at first and then I didn't. I tried to talk him out of it. I could have talked to walls or stones."

"Now, Stella."

"Don't sound soothing. Please. We've got ourselves a situation, Paul. A large one. It isn't pretty. I guessed at something of the sort . . . but not so blatant."

"We're all friends."

She turned the dark lenses toward me. "I'm your friend, Paul. I'm Jeff's friend, I hope. Not hers. Not hers, ever again. She made it plain enough. I should pack now. That would be smart. But I'm not very smart, I guess. I would rather stay and fight."

She picked up her things and went to their cottage. At noon I picked up my things and went in too. I sat on the porch and read and finally they came down the beach. They separated casually in front of our place and Linda came in.

"Long walk," I said.

She looked at me and through me. "Wasn't it, though," she said, and went on into the house.

The was the beginning. That was the way it started. Linda and Jeff were together whenever they pleased. It would, perhaps, have been better if I could have gone to Linda and demanded an explanation, if I could have shook her, struck her, raged at her. But, with Linda, the roots of my insecurity went deep. I tried to use reason.

"Linda, we planned to have a good time down here."

"Yes?"

"You and Jeff are spoiling it for the four of us. Stell is miserable."

"That's a bitter shame."

"Last night you two were gone for three hours. Not a word of excuse or explanation or anything. It's so . . . ruthless."

"Poor Paul."

"Haven't you got any sense of decency? Are you having an affair with him?"

"Why don't you run along and catch some nice fish again?"

"I can't get any pleasure out of anything I do, the way you're acting. I just don't understand it. What am I supposed to do? What's going to become of us? How can we go back and live the way we did before?"

"Do we have to, dear? Goodness, what a fate!"

It wasn't like her, not to get angry and shout and stamp her feet. She was . . . opaque. I think that is the only possible word. It was acute torture for me. I felt helpless. There seemed to be a cold precision about what they were doing that baffled me. Sometimes I felt the way you do when you walk into a movie in the middle of a very complicated feature picture. The story is incomprehensible to you. You seek a clue in the actors' words and actions, but what they do serves only to baffle you the more.

One morning I watched Jeff and Linda on the beach directly in front of our cottage. He had a carton of empty beer cans. He had the .22 and he would throw a beer can out as far as he could. He would shoot and then instruct Linda. He put his arm around her bare shoulders to get her into the proper position. I could hear the snapping of the shots over the sea sound, and once I heard their laughter. I sat and watched them and felt ill. When Linda wandered down the beach and Jeff stayed there, shooting, I went down to him. It was the first time I had been alone with him since it had started. When he looked at me his face was very still. "Hi, Paul. Want to try a shot?"

"No thanks. I want to talk to you."

He looked uncomfortable. "Sure," he said. "Go ahead."

It made me feel as though I were in a badly written play. "I guess you know what I want to talk to you about."

"I can't say that I do."

He was making it as difficult for me as he could. "It's about you and Linda, Jeff. What are you trying to do?"

"What do you mean?"

"The four of us never do anything together. You and Linda swim together, go off walking together. You're making it damn awkward for your wife and for me."

He seemed to gain confidence. "Have you talked to Linda about this?"

"Yes, I have."

"What does she say, old man?"

"Don't call me old man. She doesn't say much of anything. She won't explain or apologize. It seems to me like the most thoughtless piece of selfishness I've ever seen. It's spoiling everything. My God, if you want to break up both marriages, at least put your cards on the table."

He even smiled at me, though his eyes were still uneasy. "Paul, old man, a vacation is where you do as you please. I'm doing as I please. I guess Linda is too. So don't get so steamed up. Relax. Enjoy yourself."

He sneered a little as he said the last few words. I didn't have any tiny fragment of liking for him left. I hated him and what he was doing. Linda's personal promises had been no good. She hadn't let me touch her since we'd gotten to Florida.

I was hurt and angry. My hands and arms are hard and tough. I sprang at Jeff and hit him in the mouth. He went over onto the sand and the rifle went flying. He looked at me with complete shock which changed at once to anger as he scrambled up. I was a fool to hit him. He had the advantage in youth, in weight, height, reach and condition. The last fight I had been in had been in a schoolyard—and I had lost.

Jeff charged me with such fury that he knocked me down without actually punching me. I got up and he hit me in the chest and knocked me down again. As I got up, Stella came running between us. Instead of calling out to her husband she said to me, "No, Paul! No."

Jeff picked up the sandy rifle and stared at me and stalked toward their cabin. I saw at once what Stella meant. It didn't do any good. It couldn't do any good. Fighting over Linda was purposeless.

Back on the porch of their cottage, Jeff dismantled the rifle on spread newspapers and cleaned the sand from it with an oily rag. He was as opaque as Linda. It was a game, and neither Stella nor I knew the rules. They were both stronger people, and we did not know what to do about the strange situation. People should not act that way. They were not taunting Stella and me. They were not precisely goading me. They gave us no obvious evidence of infidelity, which would have forced it to an issue. They merely went their own casual way, as though we had changed marriage partners during the day, only to be sorted out again each night, quite late.

Stella and I were stuck with the marketing. Linda would give me a list. I would drive to Hooker and Stella would come along. Forsaking all pride, she had tried to talk to Linda. She had not wanted to weep, but she did, and hated herself for her weakness. Linda had been just as casual and noncommittal with her as Jeff had with me. It made a nightmare of what both Stella and I had hoped would be a good and happy time.

Because it was the two of us who did the shopping, the people in Hooker, as I found out later, were understandably confused as to who was married to whom. And much was later made of the fifth of November. That was the day when, as we were about to leave, Jeff asked me to get the car greased and get an oil change.

We rode to town, not talking much, both of us thinking about the two we had left behind us. It was a curious situation. We could not, in all pride, guard them and spy upon them. We left the car at a service station and walked down the hot street to a small air-conditioned bar. I suppose, as was later said, we *did* have our heads together, and we did

talk earnestly in low voices to each other. And Stella *did*
cry at one point, but very briefly.

When we got back they were both swimming about two
hundred yards offshore.

It was on Sunday, the seventh, that Stella and I went for
our walk. That was the day another distorted facet was
added to our relationship. I did not know where Linda and
Jeff were. Linda had just washed the lunch dishes and gone.
I was on the porch when Stella came over, a strained look
about her eyes. "Want to walk with me, Paul?"

"Sure." We headed south, walking briskly. "Did they go
this way?" I asked.

"No. They took the boat and went north up the bay,"
she said. "Jeff took his tackle. I just . . . want to walk,
Paul, and I didn't want to be alone."

She set a fast pace. The sun was hot on my shoulders,
but neither of us had to be so wary of the sun any more.
We were both barefoot, and she wore a strapless dark blue
bathing suit which clung to her body. It had white ruffles
at the hips and at the bodice. Her pale hair was fastened
back with a silver clip and she wore the massive dark
glasses. As I have said before, Stella is not a pretty woman.
Her brows and lashes are too pale, her nose too prominent,
her mouth too wide in her thin face.

I can quite truthfully say that until that walk I had never
looked at her as a woman, as a woman to be desired. I had
been as unconscious of her body as if she had been a
younger sister. I do not think that is due to any lack in me.
It is because I had gotten to know her as Stella, fully
clothed, in her living room at home and in mine. Even
after the transition to brief bathing suit, it was as though
I still saw her in the rather quiet clothes she preferred,
without provocative habits of walk or posture, with only
her own subdued and quiet grace.

My vision of her changed without warning, and it happened this way. We went further down the beach than I
had ever gone. We came to a place where a groyne had
been built of heavy stones to forestall erosion. The sea
had smashed it into a jagged barrier across our path.

"Turn back?" I asked.

"Let's go on." She picked her way cautiously, over the barrier. I was behind her. Her small firm hips were round under the ruffled suit. I saw the long delicacy of her legs, and the blue track of veins in the backs of her knees. Her waist was slender, her back straight. The lines of her shoulders and throat were clear and clean. When we were across and I walked beside her again I looked almost furtively at her high small breasts, the flex and lift of her thighs as she walked. I had taken her for granted, never quite looking at her, believing her body to be gaunt, bony.

Now that I was aware of her, I made inevitable comparisons. Linda was flamboyantly noticeable. Stella was subtle in the way that a Japanese print is subtle. Only after a study of the restrained delicacy of the print can you begin to see the strength and discipline and vitality of it. Linda was a portrait in heavy oils.

Do not think from this that I had begun to walk beside her drooling like a schoolboy. It was just that I noticed her for the first time and saw what she was and was saddened by it. For if Linda chose to hurt me, an action I could halfway understand through critical appraisal of myself, Jeff, in denying this woman, was doing something less understandable and more brutal. Perhaps there is always a deeper and more bitter significance when a woman is hurt. Traditionally, a man can turn to other arms, salving his ego. A woman can only wonder why the gift of herself is found not to be enough.

A half-mile beyond the rock barrier we found an old house. It had once been impressive. The flat roof had fallen in and storms had shifted plaster walls, exposing the old brick underneath. Sand had covered most of the shattered cement sea wall. Stella walked up the slope of the beach and sat on a tilted section of the sea wall. I sat beside her. Far offshore a school of bait danced and spattered in the sun as torpedo hunger smashed upward at it from deep water.

"I guess I give up, Paul," she said tonelessly.

"What will you do?"

"I don't know, exactly. Stop trying, for one thing. You

and Linda have your reservations for next Saturday, don't you?"

"That's right."

She gave me a crooked smile. "I'll use the week getting some more sun and doing some thinking. I—I never ran into anything like this. I'll let him drive me back. Maybe once they're apart he'll talk about it. Even if he was abject about it, I don't think I could stay. Not after this . . . special kind of humiliation."

She paused, then started talking very fast, not looking at me. "One summer when I was little they sent me to a very smart and exclusive camp for girls. At the camp everybody was assigned to a group of six. I arrived late. The group was all formed. I guess I was pretty discouraging to them. You see, the groups of six were in competition. Swimming and riding and so on. There I was, a wan, shy little bug-eyed thing, looking as I was made of pipe cleaners, and had a mouth full of metal and springs. They had a whole series of secrets they kept from me. They even had a special language. I had a hell of a summer. This keeps reminding me of it. I didn't know I was still so vulnerable."

I knew exactly what she meant. It surprised me because I had thought that money was always the perfect insulation against that kind of aloneness.

"Couldn't you have asked your people to take you out and send you to some other place?"

"I could have. They would have. But I didn't want to be humiliated in their eyes, either. I didn't want to seem inadequate. They both were drowned two years later, off Bimini in their boat in a storm. They were always adequate. Big brown laughing people, with white white teeth. Daddy called me the white mouse. He meant it affectionately, but it always hurt a little. Now I guess that Jeff has—has turned me back into the white . . ." She put her face in her hands. She cried silently.

I put my arm around her sun-hot shoulders, moved closer to her. I held her for a long time and when she lifted her face toward me, I kissed her, tasting salt. I took my arm away awkwardly and said, "I'm sorry."

"Don't be sorry. They threw us together. We're on the outside. We can comfort each other, I guess. Anyway, Paul, I'm glad you kissed me. It makes me feel . . . well, more competent, I guess. What are you going to do?"

"I don't know. Maybe I haven't got enough pride. I keep thinking this will blow over. Maybe it won't be precisely the same again, but it will be enough for me. I don't demand much, I guess. Or maybe merit much."

"Don't low rate yourself."

"I'm not. I'm being honest. I'm still surprised Linda married me. I guess I'm still grateful, in a sense."

She frowned and looked away from me. "Ever since I became what they coyly called marriageable, I've had a different problem. There were always plenty of them. Nice, polite, handsome, muscular young men. The thing was to decide whether it was me or the money."

"It there that much?"

"Bushels. An obscene amount. I guess I've demanded that we live simply as a sort of continuing test of Jeff. Now I wonder if that was wrong. Maybe if I'd decided it was really me he wanted, and begun to live the way we can, he wouldn't have done this. No, that wouldn't be any good either. And there's no sense in saying if I'd done this or if I'd done that. It's done now. It's over."

"Are you going to leave him?"

"Yes. And then indulge myself for a while. Play hard. Financial bandages for the bruised ego. You know, Paul, we ought to take off together. Give them back some of their own coin. Acapulco, Rome, the Virgin Islands, the south of France. A tour of the playgrounds. God, how they'd writhe!"

I looked at her. "But we can't, of course."

Her eyes were somber. "No. We can't." She stood up and tried to smile. "Back to the wars, Cowley."

We walked back to our strange war. Toward the callousness of two people who would not explain or desist. They conducted some strange campaign against us and we were helpless because we did not understand. Two white mice, perhaps. Two blind mice.

Wednesday, the tenth of November, was the hottest day of all. Though the sky was a deep and intense blue, the water was oddly gray, the swells oily, the horizon misted. There was a feel of change in the air. The day was very still, but from time to time gusts of superheated air would spin down the beach, plucking the sand up into small spirals that would die quickly as the gust faded away. A solemn army of billions of minnows moved steadily northward a few feet off the beach. Small sandpipers ran in flocks, pecking and then trotting up and away from the lap of waves, like groups of spry, stooped little men in tailcoats with their hands locked behind them.

There had been no change in either Jeff or Linda. If there was any change at all in Linda that morning, it was a slight irritability hitherto lacking, yet familiar to me, and I wondered if it foretold the beginning of the end of her strange actions. I went out onto the beach at about ten. Stella came out about fifteen minutes later, wearing a trim yellow suit. She spread her huge towel beside my blanket, went out and swam and then came back, taking her rubber cap off, shaking out her pale hair, smiling at me. She stretched out beside me and we surrendered ourselves to the hard pulse of the sun.

I heard a sharp, snapping sound and without opening my eyes I knew it was the rifle. I propped myself up on one elbow and watched Jeff shooting at the empty cans. I noticed that his eye was off. The day and the sea were so still that once I heard the skree of a ricochet when a slug skipped off the water.

Out of the corner of my eye I saw Linda coming down from our cottage. She wore, for the first time, a new swim suit which she had bought just before we left. I wondered why she had saved it until now. I wondered why she had bought it. It certainly did not become her. It was dark green, and so conservative that it looked as though she had rented it. Compared to her favorite, a wispy Bikini which seemed to be supported only by faith, this green one was practically funereal. She stood close to Jeff. He stopped shooting, bent his head a bit to listen to her. Secrets. It made me think of the white mouse in that girls' camp.

I lay back and shut my eyes. Some time later—I do not know how long, perhaps ten minutes—I opened my eyes and saw that Jeff was sitting on the other side of Stella. His long hard legs were brown, and the curled hair on them was bleached white. He sat looking out at the Gulf and I saw the knob of muscle stand out at the corner of his jaw as he clenched his teeth. I wondered what he was thinking.

It was still morning and the sun was high, though slightly in the east. A shadow fell across me. I looked down and saw the long thin shadow of the rifle barrel, the bulkier shadow of Linda. I looked back at her. She was standing behind me. She had the rifle to her shoulder and she was aiming it carefully at Stella's head. I believe that what I started to say was something to the effect that you shouldn't aim a gun at anybody, even as a macabre joke. I said half a word before Linda pulled the trigger. As the muzzle was about three feet from my face, the sound of the shot was much louder than any that had gone before.

It has been verified that the small leaden pellet struck approximately an inch above Stella Jeffries' hairline and ranged down through her skull, hydrostatic pressure of the pellet against the brain fluid bulging her face grotesquely. The pellet lodged in her throat after smashing a major artery. The immediate brain damage imparted a stimulus to the central nervous system so that her body bowed upward, resting only on her heels and the nape of her neck, rigid as iron for what seemed to me to be seconds on end, then collapsed suddenly and utterly with a small wet coughing noise that smeared suit, throat, shoulders and big towel with bright red blood.

If you have never seen an equivalent moment of bright violence, it will be impossible for you to undertand the mental and emotional results of the shock. For one thing, the actual moment itself is stamped into your mind as though hammered there by a great steel die. Imagine that each of your areas of thought is a sheet of paper, and these sheets of paper are carefully stacked, and the impact of the die embosses the picture of violence all the way down through the stack, sharply and clearly. So that later, should you think of chess or spinach, ashtrays or beef cattle, even the texture of that area of thought bears the clear-edged memory of sun and sand, of the way the long muscles of her legs pulled rigid as she bowed her body, of the way the single eye you could see, far open in the instant of death, showed white all the way around the blinded iris and pupil, of the way the hand nearest you, after the collapse and gout of blood, made one last movement, a tremor of thin fingers so slight that perhaps you didn't see it at all.

The second aspect, more difficult to describe, is the way shock makes subsequent though processes unreliable. It is as though the brain makes such a convulsive effort to take in every tiny aspect of the moment of violence that it exhausts itself and, thereafter, functions only intermittently, absorbing varied memories but interspersing them with periods of blankness impossible to recall.

When I looked, stupefied, at Linda, I saw the muzzle of the rifle swing slowly toward Jeff. She worked the bolt expertly. A tiny gleaming cartridge case arced out onto the sand.

Jeff gave a great hoarse cry of panic. I believe I shouted something at the same moment. What it was, I do not know. I tried to grab at Linda, but she moved quickly away from me. Jeff had bounded to his feet and he ran hard, ran in a straight line away from us. The rifle snapped and he plunged forward, turning his right shoulder down as he fell, rolling over twice to lie still on his face. Linda fired again with great care a fraction of a second before I grabbed the gun and twisted it out of her hands. Out of the corner of my eye I saw Jeff's body twitch as she fired.

I had the gun. She looked at me. Her eyes were like frosted glass. The lower half of her face was slack. Her underlip had fallen away from her teeth. I remember that there was a fleck of brown tobacco on one of her lower teeth and that I had the insane impulse to reach out with my finger and remove it. I do not know what was said, if anything, because at that point there came one of those blind spots in memory.

I remember standing there with the rifle in my hands. Linda had apparently walked up the beach some hundred feet. She was standing in the water, in shallow water, bending awkwardly forward and being sick. I could not look at the body of Stella or the body of Jeff. I have always been that way. Linda laughed at me one time a few years ago. During the night a cat had died in our yard. I don't know what had killed it. I could not touch it. I could not stand looking at it. I dug the hole for it and went in the house. Linda put it in the hole and covered it up.

As I walked up to Linda she reached down and brought up sea water in her cupped hands and rubbed her mouth vigorously. She looked at me and her face was the same as before. "Go . . . report it!" she said in a thickened voice.

"Come with me," I demanded.

"No."

I took her by the wrist and tugged her toward the cottages, toward the car. Partway up the beach she let herself go limp. She lay there on the sand, her eyes closed. "Come with me. You're sick," I said.

"No."

Again there was a gap in memory. I remember next getting into the car. There was something that impeded me and irritated me, and I did not realize what it was. I brought my attention to focus and found that I was sitting behind the wheel with my left hand still grasping the rifle, my fingers holding it so tightly that they were cramped. I could not shut the car door without either releasing it or bringing it inside. It was very like the infuriating obstacles which confront you when you are very drunk. I put the rifle on the back seat. I remember no aspect of the trip to Hooker. I was not thinking constructively about what should be done. Linda was sick and had committed senseless violence. Her violent temper had taken that one last step over the borderline into insanity. It was a hideous mess, and I realized vaguely that there would be no end of confusion and heartbreak. I believe that on that short drive I resolved to stand by her and convinced myself that her curious actions of the previous two weeks had been, had I only known it, the danger signal.

I parked in front of the market. The Jethro woman has given a description of the way I acted when I came in. "He come in here breathing hard and looking sort of wild. He stood looking at me and licking his lips and I askec him twice what the trouble was, and then he said his wife had shot and killed the couple in the next cottage, the other Dooley cottage. People like them, they come down here and drink and carry on and half the time they don't know what they're doing. He was in his swimming pants and it was hot in the store, but he was all over goose lumps and shivering.

"Buford Rancey was in buying bread and they got this Cowley over in a chair in the back while I phoned over to Bosworth, to the sheriff's office. They said one car was on road patrol over on the Trail, and they'd be along in maybe five minutes after they told them over the radio. This Cowley sat in the chair with his eyes shut, still shaking, still licking his mouth every once in a while. Buford Rancey gave him a cigarette and he shook so bad I thought he'd miss his mouth with it.

"The road car came roaring up in front and there was just that Dike Matthews in it. That Cowley acted a little better. Dike said as how Sheriff Vernon and some folks were on their way from the county seat, and somebody better be at the market to guide them on out. Buford said as how he would do that, so then Cowley got in the big car and Dike followed him on out. People had come in the market knowing somehow there was some kind of trouble, so there were two more cars that followed along. I'd say that twenty minutes later, after Buford had just left to ride out with Sheriff Vernon, half the town of Hooker had gone on out to Verano Key to stand around with their fool mouths open."

Because Matthews was following me in the other car, I didn't get any chance to talk to him on the way out. I pulled in front of the Jeffries cottage, wondering in that moment if I would have to pack up their things and ship them north, and wondering if I would have to drive the car north.

Matthews pulled in beside me. You can't see the beach proper from directly in front of the cottages, on the road. He was an angular man with a weather-marked face, lean throat, wattled jaw, prominent Adam's apple, narrow blue eyes.

We got out of the cars and he looked in at the back seat of Jeff's car and said, "That the weapon?"

"Yes," I said, and opened the door to get it.

"Leave it be," he said sharply. "You put it there?"

"Yes," I said.

He spat and glanced at the sky. "Well, where are they?"

"Down on the beach. We were lying in the sun. Mr. Jeffries was shooting at floating cans. My wife took the rifle. She shot Mrs. Jeffries in the head from close range. She aimed at Mr. Jeffries. He ran. She hit him and knocked him down and shot him again. I got the gun away from her. She's been . . . acting strange lately."

We walked toward the road and the beach. Two other cars had pulled up beside the road. People had gotten out. They saw where we were heading and they began to drift in the same direction.

"Killed 'em both, eh?" he said.

"Killed Mrs. Jeffries. Maybe Mr. Jeffries was only seriously wounded. But I think he was dead."

"Didn't you look?"

"No. I—I should have. But I was shocked. I went after help."

We stood on top of the sand rise and looked down at the beach. From that distance and that angle, Stella could have been sunbathing. I could see the dark glasses on the corner of her towel, see the glint of her lotion bottle in the sun. My blanket was spread out beside her body.

And that was all. Jeff's body was gone. Linda was gone. I couldn't understand it. I had all sorts of crazy conjectures.

Linda had drowned herself. Jeff had crawled up to the
cottage somehow.

We walked down toward the body. I forced myself to
look at it. When I saw the sharp circling of the flies I
looked away.

"Where's the other body?" Matthews asked.

"I don't know. Maybe he wasn't as badly hurt as I
thought."

"Where was he?"

"Right there," I said. "Right about there." I pointed.
I walked over with him. He sat on his heels and looked
at the sand. He stood up.

Six people had moved down to within twenty feet of
the body. They were all staring at the body. "Git back,
dammit. Git back!" Matthews bawled. They all moved back
a half-step, still staring. He strode over angrily, snatched
up my balled towel, snapped it out and spread it with sur-
prising delicacy over Stella's broken head.

I looked at the sand. Hot dry sand takes no tracks. The
sand spills loosely into any depression. A bare foot makes
a depression indistinguishable from that made by a shod
foot. I searched the water, far out, looking for a head.
I looked north along the deserted beach, and south to the
headland. The wide beach was empty. Terns dipped and
laughed.

"Where'd she stand?" Matthews asked me.

I stood where Linda had stood. With my towel across
Stella's face, I could bear to look at her. It was a dark
maroon towel. I remembered when Linda had bought the
set. They had been on sale. I saw a small white diamond
scar on Stella's slack knee. The body bears the marks of
life. A wound from skating, or a bold venture in a play-
ground swing. Tears and comfortings, and a scab to go
almost too tritely with the braces on her teeth. I tore my
mind away from such imaginings.

Matthews squatted beside the cartridge case which had
been ejected after Linda had shot Stella. He regarded it
somberly, sighed and stood up and spat again.

"I'll go look in the cottages," I said.

"We'll both go." Now there were eight people standing around. I had not seen the other two arrive. Matthews bullied them back and then said, "You, Fletch." A fat man in torn khaki pants nodded. "Keep 'em all back, will you? Don't let 'em stomp around none."

We went up to the cottages. Another car was stopping. The people got out and glanced at us and then hurried down to the beach. We went in our cottage first. It was empty. It felt empty. Our footsteps were loud. We looked in the other one. It was just as empty. We went in back and looked at the dock.

"What does Dooley get a month for these, this time of year?" he asked.

"A hundred and fifty apiece."

"Hmmm," he said softly. "You all friends to these Jeffries long?"

"About a year."

"Drive down together?"

"My wife and I drove. The Jeffries flew down. Got here two days after we did."

"Who owns the weapon?"

"Jeffries did."

"Bring that on the plane?"

"No. We brought their bulky stuff down in the car. It's his car, actually. He was going to drive it back and we were going to fly, leaving Saturday."

"Sort of changes all your plans."

"Yes," I said. "It does."

"Know why she up and shot them?"

"I haven't any idea. She's sick, I think."

"Any medical history of being sick like that?"

"No. None. But I guess nearly anybody can go off the deep end."

"We better get back on the beach before somebody gets the idea of looking under that towel."

I counted fifteen people on the beach. Two small boys had lost interest. They were up the beach, excavating a sand crab.

Matthews herded the others back. He sat tirelessly on his heels, quite near the body. He had picked up a small white shell. He flipped it up and caught it, flipped it up and caught it.

"I'll walk on down the beach and look," I said.

"You stay right here. Sheriff should be here by now."

Sheriff Vernon was a sick-looking man. He was heavy, short of breath, and his face was sweaty gray. Four men followed him, two of them in the uniform of the county road patrol. He shouldered through the crowd, turned on them and said, "Back!"

They moved back a few feet. "Back to the road," he said. "All the way. All of you. Whoever belongs to those kids, get them back too." His voice was like a whip. The spectators moved back sullenly, but they moved back all the way. They stood on the high mound this side of the road, outlined against the sky, watching us.

"Doc show yet?" he asked Matthews.

"Not yet."

Vernon grunted as he stooped and lifted a corner of the towel. He looked for long seconds and dropped it again. He straightened up, glanced at me and said to Matthews, "Well?"

"This here man is named Paul Cowley. He and his wife was taking their vacation together with the Jeffries in those two cottages Dooley built. He says his wife . . ."

I stopped listening. I looked to the north again, and then to the south. As I looked to the south I saw two small figures in the distance come around the headland, walking toward us, walking side by side, a man and a woman.

"Somebody coming now," Matthews said.

We all looked toward the two figures. They both began to hurry toward us. I recognized Jeff and Linda. Jeff carried a fishing rod. He began to run toward us, outdistancing Linda. I stared at him incredulously. He slowed down as he came up to the group, his face harsh with strain.

"What's happened?" he demanded. "Paul, what's the matter?"

He saw her then, beyond us. He dropped the rod and reel into the sand and plunged toward her. He fell to his knees, reached toward the towel, hesitated and then took it off. Linda had reached the group. She screamed. I turned sharply toward her as she screamed and saw the stringer drop to the sand. There were three plump sheepshead on the stringer with their gay wide black and white stripes. They began to flap around in the sand.

"What happened to her?" Jeff asked in a toneless, mechanical voice. "What did that to Stella?"

Someone took the towel from him and covered her face again. The people were moving down onto the beach again.

"She was shot in the head," Vernon said brutally.

Jeff stared at me. "Paul . . . It was an accident. Wasn't it an accident, Paul? Paul!"

He got to his feet. My mouth worked but I could not say anything. I took a step back. Linda made a sick sound in her throat, took a ragged step to the right and crumpled to the sand. Jeff came at me. His hard fist hit under my ear and knocked me sprawling. People were yelling. I was dazed. He fell on me and his hard hands closed on my throat. I grabbed his wrists and tried to pull his hands loose. He was grunting with effort. They pulled him away. I sat up, coughing and massaging my throat. Four men were clinging to Jeff's big arms. He wrenched and plunged, trying to tear free. I coughed and swallowed. My throat felt as though it was full of sand. A man had rolled Linda onto her back. He knelt beside her, massaging her wrist, watching Jeff warily.

Suddenly the fight went out of Jeff. "All right," he said woodenly. "All right, you can let go."

They released him tentatively, ready to grab again, but when he just stood there, they stepped back. "Just what in the purified hell is going on here?" Sheriff Vernon demanded bitterly. I got slowly to my feet. The whole left side of my face ached where I had been hit.

Jeff looked out toward the Gulf, his face bitter. "I guess

I can tell you," he said. "Cowley has been pestering my wife for the last two weeks. Making a fool of himself. Making clumsy passes. Stell was amused at first. I told him to lay off. He said he would, but as soon as he had a drink he'd start again. We threatened to leave. Linda— Mrs. Cowley, begged us to stay. He was better yesterday and this morning. I was going to go fishing. Linda wanted to come too. Stell said she'd stay. Cowley borrowed my rifle to do some target shooting, he said. He probably started the same old routine and Stell got annoyed. I felt uneasy leaving the two of them here. I should have come back."

I stared at him. It was like being in a nightmare. They were all looking at me. A man in uniform had eased around behind me. Linda was sitting up, looking at me with completely phony sadness.

I am positive that I looked the picture of shame and guilt. My voice was too shrill. "It wasn't that way! It wasn't that way at all! It was you, Linda, running around with Jeff. You shot her, Linda. I saw you shoot her and you shot Jeff too."

He stared at me. *"Linda* shot her! Linda's been with me for the last hour and a half. She caught two of those three fish. And you say Linda shot me, Cowley? Where? Show me where I'm shot."

Linda came up to me. She put her hands on my forearm. Her fingers were cold. She looked into my eyes. Her mouth was sad. I thought I could see little glints of triumph and amusement deep in her eyes. She looked sedate, respectable, in her severe swim suit. "Please, darling," she said. "You don't know what you're saying. Please be calm, dear."

I hit her across her lying mouth, splitting her lips and knocking her down. They jumped me. They roughed me up and handcuffed me to a man in uniform. They hustled me up to the car. Two men were getting out of a tan ambulance. A man with a black bag glanced at us and walked down toward the beach. They put me in the back seat of one of the official cars. They drove me away from there.

They spun the wheels on the sand, and screamed the tires when they were on concrete.

Bosworth, the county seat of Semulla County, was eighteen miles further south. I was officially charged with suspicion of murder, photographed, fingerprinted. I was still, incongruously, in swimming trunks, barefooted. There were no pocket items to be surrendered. They gave me a pair of gray twill coveralls much too large for me. They were clean and stiff and smelled of medicinal disinfectant. I rolled up the cuffs and turned back the sleeves. I gave my age, name, address, height, weight, date and place of birth and told them, when questioned, that I had no prior arrests or convictions. I felt as if it was all taking place behind thick glass. I watched through the glass. I could see lips move, but I could not hear clearly.

They walked me down a long hall with a cold tile floor. I could look through open doors and see girls in light blouses working at oak desks. My bare feet padded on the floor. People in the halls glanced at me with casual, knowing curiosity. They took me into a small room with a big table, five chairs, two barred windows. They pushed me into a chair. Stay there, they said.

They left a fat young man with a red face with me. He wore gray pants, a white mesh sports shirt, a black pistol belt. He sat on the table, swinging his legs, working a kitchen match back and forth from one corner of his mouth to the other.

Now I saw how all the parts went together. Nothing had made sense until the final act, and then it was all clear. I c ould enumerate all the little pieces which blended so carefully. Obviously, after we had gotten to know the Jeffries, Linda had met him clandestinely. Others too, perhaps. But I did not want to think about that. This was her big chance. What they had stolen had not been enough for them. They had to have everything. Everything in the world.

I remembered her strained silence on the way down. After she had heard the Carbonellis' description of Verano

Key, of how deserted it was out of season, she had decided on it as the perfect scene for the crime to be.

After talking it over with Jeff, she had brought it up casually while we played bridge. Jeff, according to plan, had become enthusiastic. Thus they had trapped the two of us. He had brought the gun. I remembered that it was a new one. They had spent hours alone together on the key while Stella was still alive, planning, practicing, rehearsing. Knowing they had to be alone to plan, they—or Linda—had taken the boldest way. They were confident that their two white mice wouldn't escape from the trap.

All the parts fitted. His coaching her in the use of the rifle: her aim had to be good to miss him convincingly. She knew I wouldn't go and examine him. She remembered the cat.

The people in Hooker would remember the times I had come in alone with Stella. They had even made certain of that.

Even the live fish. Sheepshead are durable. They will live overnight on a stringer in the water. Jeff had gone fishing alone, yesterday, on the bay side. I had seen him catching fiddler crabs for bait on the muddy bay beach. I had not seen him return. Obviously he had caught three fish, fastened his stringer to a low mangrove branch, hidden the rod and reel, sauntered back. Three live fish—that was a touch of art, nearly of genius.

They had known I would take the rifle away from her.

I wondered how many times they had gone over their lines. Perhaps the size of the audience surprised them a bit. Their act had not run true—not to me. But it had sounded right to the others. I could see that.

Linda had not rehearsed being sick. Perhaps that is the single thing in all of it that truly came as a surprise to her. How carefully she must have searched the beach, before turning the gun on Stella. Through the telescopic sight the hair lines would cross on that fair hair. How long did she hesitate before she pulled the trigger? Or did she hesitate not at all, while Jeff, jaw muscles bulging, body tense, sat and looked out into the Gulf, awaiting the

snapping sound of the shot which would eliminate this
wife who liked to live simply. Which would release him
into a new world where the money was his own and the
cat's-paw woman he had used to obtain the money would
also be his.

It had been easy to anticipate what the Cowley fool
would do. As soon as the car went down the road they
would hurry down the beach and cross over to the bay
side where Jeff had concealed the fish and equipment. Perhaps he came, unseen, to a place where he could watch
the beach so that their timing would be perfect—as perfect
as it was. His attack on me had been planned, and wholeheartedly murderous. It was a release for his tension, and
a chance to look good in the eyes of the law, so he had
been enthusiastic.

I wondered what he thought as he looked at the dead
face of his wife. Triumph? Sadness? A gnawing premoni-
tion that maybe it would all go wrong?

There was no point in thinking about it. The red-faced
man glanced at me. His eyes were mild, good-tempered,
speculative. "A nice mess," he said softly.

"Can I have a cigarette, please?"

He slid a pack of matches along the table to me. "Keep
the deck," he said.

I lit a cigarette gratefully. "I should have a lawyer," I
said. I was surprised that my voice was so calm.

"It might help," he said. Help was pronounced he'p.

"You live here. Could you recommend somebody?"

"Lots of times for bad trouble they get somebody all
the way out from Tampa. Some good criminal boys up
there. Me, I say Journeyman right here at home is good as
any imports. A fighter, that boy."

"Could I phone him?"

"They'll let you know as to when you can use a phone,
mister."

"What's going to happen next?"

"Well, I sort of imagine Vernon will get the reports
together and get hold of Carl Shepp—he's the county
prosecutor—and then they'll take statements from your

wife and the Jeffries fellow, and then they'll likely as not drop in here and have a chat with you."

"I don't have to talk without a lawyer, do I?"

"You don't rightly *have* to."

At two-thirty they brought me a fried egg sandwich and a coke. I was able to eat only half the sandwich. My red-faced guard ate the other half. At three they came trooping solemnly in, Vernon, a pimply female stenographer, a tall white-haired man who looked like a political poster, and a young man in a pink sports shirt with tanned powerful forearms, a face like a block of carved wood, alert eyes. Vernon glanced at me with bored professional distaste. The pimply girl stared with avid awe. The politico looked at me from stern and lofty heights of great principle. The husky young man looked at me with an alive, interested curiosity in his deep-set gray eyes.

They took chairs and Vernon said, "Cowley, this is Mr. Carl Shepp, the county prosecutor, and this is his assistant, Mr. David Hill," Vernon opened a folder in front of him and said, "Now we got to ask you some questions for the record. Anything you say may be used in evidence against you."

"May I have an attorney present, please?"

"That's your right," he said reluctantly. "We'll adjourn this session until you can locate an attorney and confer with him, Cowley."

"I don't want to confer with him in advance. I'd just as soon answer anything you ask. I just want him to be here so he can hear what's said."

"Roose," he said to my red-faced guard, who was standing by the door. "There's a list in my office of all the lawyers practicing in this area. Get it and—"

"I'd prefer a man named Journeyman," I said.

Vernon gave Roose a look of disgusted malice. "All mouth, eh? Well, phone your pal Journeyman and get him over here."

While we waited, Vernon and Shepp sat close together and looked at the folder. Vernon turned the pages. From time to time they would whisper to each other.

His name was Calvin Journeyman, and he came into the room at a full lope. The other men wore sports shirts in concession to the thick heat. Journeyman wore a rusty black suit and a pale yellow bow tie. The suit did not fit him well. Perhaps no suit could have fit him well. He had a small torso and great long spidery arms and legs. He had black hair combed straight back, a knobbly red face, and at least a full inch of sloping forehead. His eyes were the milky blue of skim milk. They flicked from face to face, came to rest on me.

"Don't let 'em lean on you, Paul," he said. "Why'nt you folks clear out in the hall a minute, let me talk to my client?"

"I'm willing to answer anything they want to ask without any previous instructions," I said.

"Go rassle another chair in here, Roose," he said to the guard. He frowned at me. "Don't like anybody to start off not taking legal advice. Anyway, we've got nothing to hide, like you say, so let it roll, Vern."

The chair was brought and he leaned back, lean fists under his chin, eyes busy. First they had me tell the story in my own words. Then Vernon took me back over it, point by point.

"You saw the shadow of the gun barrel?"

"Yes, sir."

"What did you see when you looked back?"

"I saw Linda aiming the rifle at Stella's head."

"Did the dead woman have her eyes shut?"

"Yes. She was on her back. The sun was bright."

"How far was the muzzle from the dead woman's head?"

"Five feet, perhaps. Maybe a little less."

"Did you give her cause—jealousy—to kill Mrs. Jeffries?"

"No. I told you that it was Jeff and Linda who—"

"All right. Are you familiar with that rifle?"

"Yes, sir. I've fired it at cans. I'm not a good shot."

"How many times have you driven to Hooker with Mrs. Jeffries?"

"Five or six times."

"Ever go into a place called the Crow's Nest with her?"

"Yes, sir. To kill time while the car was being greased."

"Did she cry while she was in there with you?"

"Yes, sir."

"What made her cry?"

"Well, she was upset about the way Jeff and Linda were carrying on. It was spoiling our—"

"All right. Did you on the night of October thirtieth see Mrs. Jeffries walking alone on the beach and leave the porch of your cottage and go and catch up with her and make improper advances to her?"

"No, sir."

"Did you not insist that the Jeffries take their vacation at the same time and in the same place, and do all the planning therefore?"

"No, sir. Jeffries wrote to Mr. Dooley and sent him the check and all."

"Did he not do that at your request?"

"No, sir."

The questions went on in that vein, on and on. And at last they ended. Vernon looked at me. He looked at the stenographer. "Don't take this down, honey. Cowley, you look bright enough. Just how in the hell do you expect to sell intelligent people a yarn like you dreamed up? I was there. I saw Jeffries' reaction. I saw your wife's reaction. I saw the way you looked. I know the way you acted when you went into the market there at Hooker. I've talked to your wife. She's a fine girl and you've broken her heart. I talked to Jeffries. He's just plain stunned by what you did. And you can still sit there and lie to us the way you do and keep a straight face. It isn't even a good lie. God help you."

Journeyman drawled, "You're yappin' at my client, Vern. Beats me the way you think you can tell people are lying. I remember three weeks ago Saturday you folding three eights because you thought I wasn't lying about my flush. It's as plain as the nose on your face those two smart operators have set my client up in a bind. Jeffries

gets the money and gets this boy's wife too. Know any
stronger motives than that? Lord, a man doesn't kill off a
little honeybear just 'cause he can't get aholt of it, does
he?"

"Gentlemen, I hardly think we're trying this case here,"
Carl Shepp said ponderously. He stood up. "Vern, I'd ap-
preciate your cleaning up those other details we mentioned
and bringing the file over to my office in the morning.
Dave and I will go over it and make a recommendation
as to the specific charge."

They moved me to a cell. It was surprisingly large and
clean, with heavy steel casement windows, a bed and chair
bolted to the floor, a sink and toilet, a steel shelf for personal possessions. Journeyman followed me in. The door
was slammed shut and locked and Journeyman was told
to sing out when he wanted out.

I lay on the bed. I don't think I've ever been so tired.
It felt good to get my bare feet off the cold floors. Journeyman went over and looked out the window, hands in his
hip pockets, black suit jacket hiked up.

"If you got two dollars or two million, you get the same
effort from Journeyman," he said. "But it's nice to know.
What have you got?"

"I make eight thousand. I've got at least seven thousand equity in a house, a car worth about five hundred
and about twenty-one hundred savings."

He came over and stood by the bed and looked down at
me. "Paul, did you kill that woman? Now don't answer
right away. What would happen if lawyers in this country
didn't defend guilty folk? Whole judicial system would
go to smash. I've seen a hell of a lot. If you killed her, it
won't prejudice me against you, boy."

"I didn't kill her. If I had, I'd tell you. It happened exactly the way I told them downstairs."

"That story is no damn good," he said.

"It's the truth. It has to be good."

"Being the truth doesn't make it good. Being the truth
doesn't make it useful. That's the damnedest sorriest story

I ever heard. I can't take a thing like that into court. You want to get out of this or don't you?"

"I want to get out of it."

"All right, then. Anything else we could use. The gun jammed. You were trying to free it. It was pointed at her head. You've been scared so bad you've been lying ever since."

"No," I said.

"Everything went black and when you woke up, there she was."

"No."

"It was a suicide pact and you lost your nerve."

I got up off the bed. I've always been mild. I didn't feel mild then. I don't think I've ever talked louder to a human being. "No! None of that stuff. Because you know what it means? It might possibly get me in the clear, or a short sentence or something, but it gets the two of them all the way in the clear. Can't you understand that? They plotted it and did it and they want to get way with it. If I get clear I'll have to go after them and kill both of them. If I get a short sentence it will be the same. They thought I was a damn white mouse. I'm not. The only thing I'll go into court with will be the truth, and if you don't want to take the case, somebody else will."

He waited a long time, until I had cooled down. "You just better think it over, Paul. Stick with this and the whole sovereign state of Florida is going to fall on your head like it fell off a cliff."

"So I can't—"

"Shut up. Your story is so wild they're going to bring down some people to give you some tests and make sure you're sane enough to try. Do you want to save yourself, or do you want to be some kind of martyr. Don't answer now. Think it over. I've got some checking to do. I'll see you sometime tomorrow."

After he left and I was alone I knew that he was both right and wrong. Right in that it was my testimony against theirs, and I was the introvert. They were the extroverts. On the stand I would sweat and stammer and shake, and should I say the sun would rise tomorrow, it would sound like a lie. Jeffries, rugged, clean-cut, saddened, manly, would convince them. I knew in advance how Linda would be. As my wife she could not be forced to testify against me. But she could volunteer her testimony. She would try to make it look as though she were standing by me. And would damn me, while she smiled sadly.

I wondered why I had not thought of all this before—of how justice and truth are so unpredictably subject to the stage presence of the accused. I knew that Linda and Jeff had thought of it.

Waking up from an illusion is always painful, and often something that takes a long time. My awakening from the illusion of Linda had been painful, but quick. It had happened in a fraction of a second, during that moment after her contrived faint when she put her hands on my arm and I had looked into her eyes. Living with evil does not make it more apparent. I could now look back over the years of Linda and see all the things that I had misinterpreted because I had looked at them through the distorting glass of my own gratitude to her.

That night it was a long time before I could get to sleep.

AFTER THE MORNING MEAL I WAS TOLD THAT Linda had come to visit me and had brought things for me. My first impulse was to tell them to have her leave the things and go. But I was curious about her, about how she would carry it off. Visiting me was something she had to do to preserve the illusion of the story the two of them had plotted.

She came with clothing over her arm, with cigarettes and magazines and the portable radio. She wore a plain dark dress and very little make-up. The jailer was very courtly with her.

"Now you can go right in, Mrs. Cowley, and I'll be back in a half-hour. That's all that's allowed."

I sat on the bed and watched her. "Dear, they told me you could have clothes, but no belt or shoelaces, so I brought the slacks that don't need a belt, and your moccasins. Here's the socks and underwear. I'll just put them right here on this shelf. I guess the cigarettes and magazines can go here too." She put the clothing on the bed beside me and sat down in the single chair, smiled briefly at me and dug into her purse for her own cigarettes.

"I've been talking to Mr. Journeyman, dear. The county is having two specialists come down from Tampa to examine you. They should be here this afternoon, they say. I think it's for the best. You haven't acted like yourself for months."

"Keep right on. It's almost amusing, Linda."

"I've let everyone know, dear, that I'm going to stand by you no matter what you did. It was a terrible thing, but you were ill, dear. You didn't know what you were doing. I'm not going to permit myself to be annoyed or hurt by the fantastic tale you've been telling them about me."

I looked at her soft tan throat. I could reach it in two quick steps.

"I suppose Jeff is heartbroken," I said.

"He's had a terrible shock. The funeral will be on Saturday, in Hartford. We've both had a terrible time with the reporters. They've been so persistent."

"But they got your story, of course."

"You can't just refuse to say anything," she said, a bit smugly. "Jeff is leaving tonight with the body, by train. He'll have to stay up there a little while. There are a lot of legal details, I understand."

"The will, I suppose."

"Yes, and the trust funds. That sort of thing. You'd understand more about that than I would, Paul."

"Where are you staying?"

"I'm still at the cottage. The rent is paid so I might just as well stay there, don't you think? Or would you rather have me here in town, dear?"

"You're incredible, Linda. Incredible."

"I'm only doing what I think is right," she said. "They say that if these men from Tampa say you are sane, the trial will be in January. I think you ought to talk to Mr. Journeyman about our own financial arrangements, dear. He could probably arrange about having somebody up there put our house on the market and sell the car and so on. We'll need money to fight this thing, dear, if they say you are sane."

"Doesn't it mean anything to you, Linda? Didn't it change something inside of you, pulling that trigger and seeing what it did to her?"

She closed her eyes for a portion of a second. "Don't be irrational, darling," she said calmly.

"How long have you looked for the big chance? How many years? What made you think this was it? You're a damn fool, Linda. Even if it works, it won't really work, you know. He knows what you did. And that means he knows what you are. Maybe you can hold him for a little while, but the years are hardening and coarsening you, Linda. And your looks are the only thing to hold him with. You haven't got anything else. You did the actual deed, not him. He'll think about that more and more as time goes by. I suppose you plan to marry him. Maybe, right now, he's thinking how foolish that would be. It wouldn't give him anything he hasn't already had. It would be a nice joke on you, Linda. You set him free, and he leaves you flat. You wouldn't dare object. You wouldn't dare open your mouth."

She stood up abruptly. Her face was a mask. I saw that I had touched her. I saw the effort it took for her to relax again. Then she smiled. "Dear, you must get that fantasy out of your head. Poor Jeff. This tragedy has made him quite dependent on me." She gave a subtle emphasis to the word "dependent."

"You better go, Linda."

She wouldn't call the jailer. I yelled for him. He came, let her out. She turned in the open door and said, for his benefit, "Please try to get some sleep, darling. You'll feel so much better if you get some sleep."

I cursed her quietly and the jailer looked at me with pained indignation and slammed the cell door with clanging emphasis. When they were gone I undressed, washed at the sink, put on the fresh clothing. It felt good to have shoes on.

They took me to an office in the afternoon and gave me written and oral tests that lasted over two hours. A half-hour after I was back in the cell, Journeyman came in. He looked bitter. "You're sane, all right. Know what you've got? A very stable personality and good intelligence."

"What makes you so happy?" I asked him.

"All your prints they found on the gun. Plus some of Jeffries' and some of your wife's. But mostly yours. And Jeffries showed Vern where he and your wife caught the fish. Vern picked up four of her cigarette butts there, on the bank, with her lipstick on them. They fished in a hole near an old broken-down dock behind a mangrove point, so they weren't seen by any of the boat traffic on the bay. It comes down to this, Paul. It's your word against theirs. And a jury will believe them. Change your mind since yesterday?"

"No."

He roamed around the cell, hands crammed in his pockets, head lowered, scuffing his feet, whistling tonelessly. He stopped and sighed. "Okay. I'll do every damn thing I can. Shepp has decided to make a try for first degree. He'll handle it himself. Voice like an organ. Makes them cry. Well, hell. We'll do what we can."

He said he would come back the next day and go over a lot of stuff in detail, and left.

David Hill arrived at eight o'clock. He wore a big briar pipe. He looked through the bars at me and said, "I'm the opposition, so you don't have to talk to me, Cowley."

"I don't mind," I said.

He sat in the straight chair, thumbed his pipe, got it going again. "I'm a stranger here myself," he said. "I came down three years ago. Used to practice in Michigan. Passed the Florida bar, set up here and got appointed as Shepp's assistant. The doctors said my little girl would do better in this climate. Asthma. Ever play chess, Cowley?"

"No."

"When your opponent launches an attack, you must watch the moves he makes and try to figure out what he has in mind. The most nonsensical-looking moves can sometimes conceal a very strong attack."

"I'm afraid I don't follow."

"We paid per diem to two men who confirmed what I'd already guessed. You're intelligent, stable. I spent some more county funds today and talked to a man named Rufus Stick. I have a fair idea of what you're like, Cowley. You are my opponent, let's say, and I see you making a nonsensical move. In other words, your story of what happened on the beach. You stand up to stiff questioning, and they don't trip you once. So I have two assumptions. One, you made up that story and went over it in your mind until you were letter perfect on it. Two, it was the truth. Now why would an opponent I know to be able, devise a story which practically means suicide? Answer: he wouldn't. Conclusion: he told the truth. Next step, a closer look at the two other principals. How did you meet your wife, Cowley?"

I told him everything I could remember about her, and everything I knew about Brandon Jeffries. From time to time he wrote things down in a small notebook. It took a long time.

When at last he stood up to go I said, "It is the truth, you know."

He looked into his dead pipe. "I think it is, Cowley. I'll wire Jeffries to be back for the inquest. He was told his statement would be enough. I'll get him back here."

"What will you do?"

"I don't know yet." He looked at me and his face changed. "If your story is true, it's the coldest, most brutal, most callous murder I've ever heard of."

Journeyman was in the next day and we worked for three hours. Linda came the next day with more cigarettes and reading matter. I refused to see her and the jailer sullenly brought me the things she had purchased. This was Saturday, the day we were to have left, the day they were lowering the body of Stella Jeffries into the ancient soil of Connecticut. No one came to see me on Sunday. I had read everything at hand. It was a long day.

David Hill, complete with pipe, came at noon on Monday. He seemed ill at ease, as though he had to bring up something unpleasant. When he finally brought it up, it was not as unpleasant as it would have seemed a week before. It was about Linda.

"It's a good firm," he said. "We used to use them when I was in Michigan. They have an office in Los Angeles and they have a big staff, so things move fast. I had to use my own money for this."

"I'll pay you back, of course."

"Her name was still Willestone when she went out there. She went out there with a married man. He left her. She was calling herself Mrs. Brady when you met her again. Mrs. Julius Brady, you said. There is no marriage record. She lived in San Bernardino with a petty gambler named Julius Brady for a while. He cheated some soldiers at Camp Anza and was sent up. There's a blank, and then she turned up in Bakersfield, calling herself Linda Brady. She was sentenced twice there, thirty-day terms, for soliciting. She moved up to Los Angeles and was picked up in the company of a man wanted on suspicion of armed robbery. They found she was sick and committed her to the county hospital until she was well. Then she was warned to leave the city. That was about three months before you met her on the street. It—it isn't pretty, Cowley."

I thought of how she had been, years ago. I looked beyond Hill. "In school," I said softly, "she was the prettiest, and the best. Life was going to give her all the wonderful things. You could see that, just looking at her."

"Maybe she thought so too," Hill said. "Life didn't give them to her and she tried to take them, and her methods were wrong, and she got licked, beaten down. Then you picked her up and brushed her off. This time she waited for the long chance. The big chance."

"This time maybe she's made it."

"I don't think so. I don't think so at all."

"How about Jeffries?"

"Nothing on him. Orphaned. Brought up by an aunt. Never much money. Good athlete. He was working on a cruise ship—something to do with games and recreation —when he met his wife. She steered him into sales, and he did well. Her people objected at first, but finally came around. He'll be back tonight. He's flying in. I've wangled a delay on the inquest."

"Why? What can you do?"

"I don't know. They both know they'll hang together if anybody slips. They'll be careful. I've gone over it a hundred times. They did a good job. There aren't any loose ends. You said you don't play chess, didn't you?"

"I don't."

"Sometimes you see an attack shaping up. It's flawless. If you make all the expected moves, you're going to be slowly and inevitably defeated. So you don't make the expected moves. You make a wild move. It's meaningless. But they don't know positively that it's meaningless. So they have to guard against the unknown. Sometimes it can put a strong attack off balance, just enough."

After he left I thought about what he had said. Though I didn't understand how it worked on a chess board, I thought I knew how it worked in life. I could even relate it, in a small way, to my own experiences.

They had the plot and the plan and the program. They were the ones—Linda and Jeff—who had moved. I was the one who was being whirled down the careful channel they had dug to the inevitable destination they had planned for me. I paced for a time and then I sat down and made a careful evaluation of my actions. What did they expect me to do? Obviously, I was expected to sit in this cell and insist that my story was the true one, and so instruct my lawyer, and wait calmly for a trial that would end me.

Just so long as I kept to the pattern, they would feel calm. Should there be any deviation from the pattern, they would begin to feel uneasy.

I wondered how I could deviate from the pattern. The most obvious idea was to escape. I discarded that at once. It was idiotic. Meaningless.

Yet David Hill had spoken of the meaningless move. And how the opponent must guard against the unknown. Purely as an intellectual game, it would hurt nothing to think of escape. It startled me a little to find that I could contemplate it even as a game. Linda had indeed changed me.

I knew that my cell was on the top floor. There were two cells to the left of the guardroom, of which this was one. The other was empty. Beyond the guardroom, on the other end of the corridor, were a drunk tank and a row of smaller cells. There were three stories and a basement. No elevators. To reach the stairs it would be necessary to go through the guardroom. I had no idea of who might be in there, or even if there was always somebody there. My radio was plugged in. I turned it up higher and examined the windows. They were casement windows worked by interior cranks. The mesh screen inside was heavy. They would open only so far, not far enough to squeeze through, even if I could cut the heavy screening. And the panes were small.

It had to be through the door, if at all. My mind moves somewhat ponderously, but with logic. I could not see myself going out armed, cowing the guards. They would not let me walk out, at least not as Paul Cowley, slayer. I would either have to be someone else, or invisible. Disguising myself presented almost insurmountable difficulties. I put that line of thought aside and addressed myself to the problem of the cell door.

In spite of the massive look of the door, the lock did not seem impressive. The jailer used two keys to open the door. One unlocked a flap arrangement which covered the second keyhole, thus preventing the prisoner from reaching through the bars and trying to pick the main lock. When he closed the cell door, the main lock snapped into place, and then he used his key just for the outer flap arrangement. The door fitted closely, but in the small crack I could see the brass gleam of the metal that engaged the slot in the steel frame. Each time he pulled the door shut, he would give it a shake to test it.

It was not until an hour after darkness that I had the vague stirring of an idea of how to cheat the lock. As it was a spring lock, I suspected that the force which held the brass portion in the slot was not great. It would resist great lateral force, of course, but if it could be pushed from behind . . .

At breakfast on Tuesday I was able to get a better look at the mechanism. During the morning, by sliding a piece of paper down the crack, I was able to get an accurate idea of the dimensions of the orifice in the steel frame. Later in the afternoon, after another discouraging visit from Journeyman, I took the back off the portable radio. I had to use one prong of the plug as a screwdriver. It would not fit the screw heads until I had rubbed it to a smaller dimension on the rough wall. I disabled the radio, taking out what I decided I needed—one short length of tough wire, a longer length of flexible wire. To break the tough wire to the length I wanted, I had to hold it in my teeth and wind it around and around until it snapped. I bent the short length into a U with square corners, the approximate size of the lock orifice. I knew the bolt was loose in the orifice by the way it chattered when the jailer tested the door each time. It took a long time to fasten the longer, more flexible wire to the small piece. I had removed a small thin plate from the interior of the radio. I put the back back on.

During the afternoon I opened the back of the toilet, removed the rubber valve stop and gouged a small piece off it. I heated it with my matches, and when it bubbled and was sticky, I smeared it liberally on the small U-shaped piece of wire. An hour later it was still satisfactorily sticky to the touch. I managed with great difficulty to separate a six-inch piece of the rubber plug-in cord of the radio and peel back the insulation on both ends.

I was ready then, though not yet committed. It had seemed merely an interesting problem in mechanics. My uncommunicative jailer would visit me for the last time when he came to take away the dinner plate and spoon. Usually I passed them between the bars after, at his orders, scraping what I didn't eat into the toilet.

I left the moment of decision until the very last moment. I even reached for the plate and spoon and then slumped back on the bed. He yelled at me in irritation and then came in. I moved slowly toward the cell door. My right hand was in front of me. I slipped the U-shaped bit of wire into the orifice and pressed it in tightly just as he yelled at me. I turned back and he told me to stay away from the door. I was certain he would see the length of flexible wire that hung down from the U-shaped piece. But he was too angry to be observant.

He clashed the door shut, mumbling. He went away and I let out a deep breath. After the guardroom door closed, I fished the hanging piece of wire out with a scrap of paper. When I held it in my hand, I had in effect a line fastened to a hook, with the hook firmly around the bolt. I held the thin plate in my left hand, the wire in my right. I exerted a steady pressure. The bolt slid easily back. I slipped the plate in quickly. The wire pulled free. The bolt spring held the plate in place. The door was unlocked. I stretched out. If any visitor had come, I would have had to snatch the plate out. The bolt would have clicked into place, and I would have had it to do over again. But no one came. The darkness came slowly. I waited until midnight. By pressing my cheek against the bars I could see the strip of light under the guardroom door. I had heard no rumble of conversation in a long time. The odds were that only one man was in the room.

I took the six-inch piece of insulated wire and shorted out the wall plug. Had the guardroom been on a different circuit, I would have had to start over again with another plan. I ran to the door and looked again. The strip of light was gone. I opened the cell door, catching the plate before it could fall. I closed the cell door and the lock clicked into place. The wire I had used was in my pocket.

I hurried silently up the dark hall. The guardroom door opened inward onto the corridor, I remembered. I flattened myself against the wall beside the door. I heard somebody kick a chair in the darkness and curse. I saw a flickering

light under the door. I had expected to feel shaken, jittery.
I felt absolutely cold, and absolutely certain of myself.

The door opened suddenly, swinging back and snubbing
against the toe of my moccasin. The night jailer walked
grumbling along the corridor, shielding a match flame. Ten
feet beyond me the match went out. I went through the
dark doorway and turned to the right, crossed the small
room cautiously, found the knob and opened the door to
the main corridor. There was a light at the far end. The
staircase was shadowy. I went down as quietly as I could.
On the main floor I could hear someone typing. I went
in the opposite direction. I found an unlocked door and
went in. Streetlights outside illuminated the orderly rows
of desks and filing cabinets. I slid one of the big windows
open. It made a great deal of noise. It was a six-foot drop
into shrubbery. I landed and hit my chin on my knee, bit-
ing my lip until it bled. I ran across the midnight expanse
of the courthouse lawn, keeping to the shadow. I thought I
could hear hoarse yelling behind me. I stopped, oriented
myself, and turned north.

Every time a car passed, I moved back onto dark lawns,
crouching behind bushes. I heard a siren, back where I
had come from. I felt slightly hysterical suddenly and made
a grotesque giggling sound. This could not be Paul Cowley,
that bold slayer of crab grass, that desperate man who always says pardon me when you step on his foot, that
desperado of the cellar workshop, that pirate of the purchasing section. The siren faded and then I heard it again,
further away.

Hill had indirectly recommended a senseless move. I had
really made one.

At the north edge of town I came upon a rustic bar
set back from the road. Local cars were thick around it. I
moved in on the cars in shadow and felt through open
windows for ignition keys. A girl spoke, quite near at
hand, and a man answered her. I crouched down. I realized,
after a moment, that they were in a parked car, and only
luck had kept them from seeing me. I wanted to be out of
sight. I found a pickup truck. I crawled cautiously into the

back, found a tarp and pulled it over me. The tarp smelled
of ancient fish.

It was at least a half-hour before people got into the
truck. Two young boys, I judged. They backed out briskly.
I held my breath. They turned north. The road was smooth
and they drove fast. The wind whistled, tugged at the
corners of the tarp. I tried to make an estimate of the
miles. Suddenly the truck began to slow down. I risked
looking. The truck was slowing down to turn into a drive-
way out in the country. A single light was on in a house
set back under the pines. I thrust the tarp aside and, as
the truck made the turn, I vaulted out into the wide shallow
ditch and fell headlong. I rolled onto my back and looked
at the stars. Mosquitoes whined around my ears. A truck
rumbled by. When I looked again the house light was out.
I got up and began to walk north. I walked spiritlessly,
forcing myself. I was one of those children's toys powered
by a coil spring. The spring had been wound up tightly,
and now all the force was gone.

I had never done anything remotely like this. Perhaps
I had assumed that I would be like men I had read about,
tireless because of their anger and desperation. But I wanted
to lie down in the ditch, or flag a car headed south. My
feet hurt and I felt cross and tired. My bites itched. I
plodded along through the night, feeling dulled and purposeless. For back of me I heard the thin lost whine of a
siren, coming closer. I walked as before, telling myself I
didn't give a damn.

Then unexpected fear made me come alive. I plunged
across the ditch and tripped and fell flat. I rolled into deeper
shelter. The siren, on a high sustained note, screamed by
and faded into the north. This could not possibly be me,
this man who hid like an animal and heard, in the stillness,
the quick hard beating of his own heart. That other Paul
Cowley could never do this. Yet maybe he had ceased to
exist when the finger had pulled the trigger. Perhaps the
ridiculously small lead pellet had killed him as expertly as
it had killed all that was Stella Jeffries.

I had no watch. I guessed it could be nearly four when

I reached the turnoff to Verano Key. My eyes had adjusted to the night. I walked a half-mile down the sand road to the old wooden bridge. I stopped and listened. I could hear no far-off sound of a car. I did not want to be caught on the bridge. I ran across and turned into coarse grass and crouched on one knee, listening again. Far down the bay I could see the Coleman lights of the commercial fishermen spreading gill nets for mullet. Linda would be a mile down the key. I wondered if she slept calmly, quietly, without regret or conscience.

I trudged down the key road. From time to time I could see the night Gulf, inky under the sky, with a starlit paleness where small waves broke on the even paler sand. A shell worked its way into my left moccasin and I took it off, dumped the sand out of it. I realized that I was walking more slowly. I had no idea what to do once I arrived at the cottage.

I saw headlights ahead of me, rounding a bend in the sand road. I ran up over the sand bank to my right and stretched out. The car lurched by. It had a noisy motor, and I heard gear clattering on metal. I went back up onto the road. Finally I knew I was close. I rounded the last bend and I could see the two cottages. There were lights on in the near one, the Jeffries cottage. I stood for a moment, then turned abruptly to the left, forcing my way through the heavy jungly growth. The footing was bad, at places it was so thick I could not force my way through and had to detour. I moved as quietly as I could. I worked my way with difficulty over the tangle of mangrove roots near the water line. The bay stretched back in front of me, stars quivering on the surface of it. I stepped slowly into the warm water, moved out until I was five or six feet from the overgrown shore line. My shoes sank deeply into the mud with each cautious step.

A glitter and splash close at hand stopped me in my tracks, heart thumping. A fish had jumped. The spreading ripples made the star reflections dance. Far off I heard the commercial fishermen beating on the wooden sides of the boats, to frighten the encircled school into darting into the gill nets.

After about two hundred feet of cautious progress I saw the cottage lights on the water, making the dock visible to me. I stopped in the shadows and wondered how I could get closer. The far side of the dock was in darkness. I waded slowly out until the water was up to my chest. I lowered myself, swam with a noiseless side stroke, rounding the far end of the dock. I came in, in the darkness, until my knee struck bottom. I crawled, dripping, keeping below the level of the dock. I reached the overturned boat. I lay beside it on my back, got my arms braced and tilted it up. I eased under it, let it down slowly. The upcurve of the bow rested against the ground, so that there were two or three inches of free space on either side of me.

As I had worked at the boat, I had heard voices. Now I stretched out, waited until my breath quieted and then tried to listen. I could make out the timbre of Linda's voice, but no word that she said. There were two men. I knew I could not risk trying to get closer.

Suddenly I heard the brisk slap of a screen door and realized they had been talking on the front porch of the Jeffries cottage. I recognized the voice of the man called Dike Matthews as he said, raising his voice a bit, "Like I said, there's no need to get the jitters about it. He hasn't got a gun, and you look like you could handle him, Mr. Jeffries. Besides, I don't figure he'd head for here. What would be the point? Unless he's nuts like some folks think, in spite of what those fancy doctors said. I suspect you can go on back to sleep and not give it another thought. We got the state boys co-operating and road blocks out, and by first light they ought to pick him up."

"You'll let us know," Linda said. I realized she had moved out into the yard too. There was tension in her voice.

"Sure. We'll let you know."

"We'll come on in in the morning," Jeff said.

"Folks down there'd give a lot to know how he got the

hell out of a locked cell. The lock works fine. They been testing it and scratching their heads."

"He was always clever with his hands," Linda said. It gave me a strange feeling to hear her speak of me in the past tense. As if what they plotted for me had already happened. As if I were dead—a man she had once been married to.

A starter whined and the car motor caught and roared. The headlights swept across the boat as he backed out. I heard the car go on down the sand road. I listened for the sound of the screen door again to indicate they had gone back in. Linda said something I could not catch.

"I just don't like it, that's all!" Jeff said. "I don't like any part of it." His voice was pitched higher than usual. It was querulous. "As far as I'm concerned, I'd like to get in the car and go find a motel where—"

"Shut up! Shut up!" she said violently. "Good lord, do you think he's going to pounce out from behind a bush or something?"

"No, but—"

"Will you *please* be quiet?"

"But we didn't—"

"Come here," she said. I heard the scuff of their feet on the grass as they came toward the overturned boat. They walked by the boat in silence. I heard the sound of their steps on the wooden boards of the dock. At the same time I heard the distant rumble as Matthews, on his way back, drove over the loose boards of the bridge a mile away.

They stopped so close to me that I could hear him sigh. I worked my way close to the edge of the boat, got my eye to the crack. They sat side by side on the dock, their legs hanging over the water. She wore her bulky white beach robe. The match flame illuminated their faces.

"Tomorrow," she said in a low tone, "you're going to move to Bosworth. It wasn't smart to move back into that cottage. I'll stay here. We were stupid to give anybody the chance to make any guesses about us."

"He didn't suspect anything. Why don't we go up to the house? It's too buggy out here."

"We don't go up to the house because I want to talk to you. I had to be away from the cottage several times. One of them, the young one named Hill, keeps starting the wrong kind of conversation. I don't like the way he looks at me. And I'm playing this safe, Jeff. Terribly safe. He could have put something in the cottage, either cottage, so he could record what we said. That's all right so long as we stick to our agreement always to talk about it as if Paul did it, but not now, not this way."

"That Matthews didn't suspect anything," Jeff said sullenly.

"And if he didn't, whose fault was that? I'm the one who heard him drive in. I'm the one who had to make the mad dash across the yard while you answered the door. You move into town tomorrow."

"All right, all right. But I don't like all this. Why did he break out?"

"Can't you see it's the best thing that could have happened? They'll catch him and they'll all think he escaped and tried to run because he's guilty. He won't have the ghost of a chance after this."

"But I keep thinking that he thought of something we didn't think of. Paul's no dummy. You ought to know that. Suppose he came back here to check on something that we overlooked?"

"You kept telling me you had good nerves. Sure. Nothing could rattle you. Just plan it all out and then sit tight. No loose ends."

"But—"

"But nothing. What could go wrong? Use your thick head. We even thought of putting cigarette butts down there with my lipstick on them proving that I spent time there with you. There was no one on the beach, no one out in a boat, who could possibly have seen what happened. If you could just see the way they treat me down there. I'm the loyal wife being brave about everything. I'm so demure it sickens me."

There was a long silence. I heard a butt hiss as it was flipped into the water. He said, "I didn't know it would be

—the way it was. I guess I thought she'd just look as if she were asleep. But her eyes . . . and the blood . . ."

"Shut up!"

"Stop telling me to shut up!"

I sensed the effort behind her calm voice. "Jeff, darling, I'm sorry. I just don't want you to think about that. I—I have to think about it too, you know."

"Yes, you really have to think about it, don't you?"

"Now don't start that. From the point of view of the law, my friend, it was our finger on that trigger, not just mine. Ours. Please, Jeff. Try to take it easy. Nothing can happen to us. We planned it too carefully. And don't fret about Paul. He hasn't got the guts of a rabbit. All we have to do is wait and act sad and co-operate with them. When it's all over, we'll wait a reasonable period of time and then we can be together."

"On her money."

"Wasn't that the object?"

"Hell, I don't know. I don't know anything any more. I just wish we hadn't done it. I just wish I could turn some magic clock backwards and we'd all be there on the beach and—"

"You can't."

"I know."

"It's done and we have to do what we said we'd do and then we'll be safe."

"And all we have to do is live with it."

"Honestly, I . . . You better go to bed. And lock all your doors and windows and put the pillow over your head."

"That wasn't necessary."

"You make me so sick sometimes. Good night, Jeff."

I heard him get up. "You better come and get your clothes," he said.

"I'll get them in the morning," she said tonelessly.

He walked by the boat. I heard the screen door slam a few moments later. She lighted another cigarette. I wondered what she was thinking about, sitting there, looking out at the black water. Was she seeing Stella's face too, as I was, as Jeff was? Or did it mean nothing to her? Was she ice all the way through, inhuman, inexplicable? This creature had shared my bed, and I thought I knew her better than any other person had ever known her. And yet I had known nothing about her.

The lights in the Jeffries' cottage went out. I heard her walk by the boat. I could have reached out, caught her ankle, brought her down to where I could reach her throat. I could think of that, yet I could not do it. She knew about the rabbit in me. She was safe in the black night.

By gray dawn I had decided. The trap was too perfect. There was no flaw. They would punish themselves. Murder was the bond on which they were going to try to build a life. They were hostage to each other, and one day—perhaps inevitably—there would be murder again.

I did not know how far I could get. I did not care very much. With luck I could find a new place, work with my hands, try to forget all this. I lifted the boat, wriggled out, walked boldly between the two sleeping cottages out to the sand road. The big car sat heavy in the dawn light, windows misted. I looked down at the beach where Stella had died. Porpoise rolled a hundred yards offshore. I walked north to the bridge and crossed it. There were no cars. I decided to turn toward Hooker. I could cut across country behind the town and head on north.

I was fifty feet beyond the bridge when the harsh voice behind me said, "Cowley!"

I stopped. They told me to clasp my hands on top of my head. I did so. The one with the rifle was Dike Matthews. I did not know the other one. I found out later that they had been waiting below the bridge, out of sight. They had not stopped me on the bridge for fear I would leap the rail into the channel. The car was up on the shoulder of the main road. They manacled my hands and walked behind me. My shoes were still wet, and made squelching sounds. They would let me walk about four steps before they would shove me hard, so I would stumble forward. They shoved me into the car. Matthews called in to say he had picked me up. Then he drove at breakneck speed back to the

cottages to see what harm I might have done Linda and
Jeff. They came out, blinking with sleep and surprise. I saw
the confidence flow back into Jeff's face as he looked at
me. I looked away.

Linda said, "No, he didn't come here at all. Thanks for
letting us know. I guess this proves how sick he is."

They took me back. A photographer snapped pictures
of me as fast as he could change bulbs and plates as they
took me into the county building. They didn't unmanacle
me until they had shoved me into the cell opposite the
one I had escaped from. Vernon came and asked questions.
Journeyman came and talked to me. I answered neither
of them. I had begun to understand that peculiar psychology of the criminal which enables him to close an unseen
door, closing out the world. I had nothing to say to them,
and no interest in what they were saying to me. Their words
came from far away, and meant nothing.

I was sleeping heavily when David Hill arrived. When
I awakened he was in the cell, smoking quietly, watching
me. He took the pipe out of his mouth and grinned, said,
"I was the one who was going to make an unexpected move,
not you."

"It didn't do any good," I said. It was the first time
I had spoken since my capture.

"What did you do?"

I told him. I told him how I had gimmicked the lock,
how I had gotten out, about the ride in the truck, the long
walk, hiding under the boat. I told him, as nearly as I could
remember, what had been said. I told him how they had
grabbed me near the bridge.

He filled his pipe again, lit it carefully. "I might have
had a few small doubts before," he said. "But now I know
you're innocent, Cowley."

"How do you know that?"

"You're a steady and logical man, but you're not very
imaginative. You scored low on that. You had a hell of a
job at those ink blots and seeing anything other than an
ink blot. It would take a pretty active creative imagination
to make up the conversation you've just told me. That's

good enough proof, to me, but not to anybody else. Not
to Vernon or Shepp or any of them. They'd laugh in my
face. Those jokers would have to have an actual playback
of that conversation before they'd buy it. Then they'd be
reluctant."

"She was afraid somebody had wired the cottages, somehow. I wish I'd had some kind of tape recorder or something with me. Then that nonsensical escape would have
worked."

He looked at me for a long time, the pipe motionless in
his hand, two deep wrinkles between his eyebrows. "Told
anybody else about this?" he asked.

"No."

He got up and paced back and forth. From time to time
he would stop and look at nothing, and then pace again.

"It's worth a try, anyway," he said.

"What's worth a try?"

"You did have a tape recorder with you. But first I have
to do one hell of a sales job on Vernon and Shepp."

It took him over an hour. He came back with paper,
a clip board, pencils. He pretended to snap sweat off his
brow. "A sales job indeed," he said. "According to them
I am, at best, a dreamer, a sucker, a soft-head. I pulled out
all the stops. Indignant, servile, haughty, scornful. In effect,
I've bet my job on you, Paul."

"I don't think you should—"

"Here. Start writing. I want the script of that talk. Every
damn word you can remember."

I took the pencil and looked at the empty paper. "I
can't remember," I said.

"Look. You're under a boat. It's dark. You're soaking
wet. They walk by you, close enough to talk. They sit on
the dock. Who spoke first?"

I looked at the paper. I put down on "L" to indicate
Linda, put a dash after it and wrote, "Tomorrow you're
going to move to Bosworth. It wasn't smart to move back
here." I looked at Hill. I said, "I don't know if that was
the exact wording or not."

"Is it the way she *could* have said it? Is it in character?"

"Yes, but—"

"What makes you think their memories will be better than yours? Write what they said. Keep is as close as you can."

I wrote, "I'll stay here. We were stupid to give anybody a chance to guess anything about us."

J— "He didn't suspect anything. It's buggy here. Why don't we go up to the cottage?"

HE LEFT ME ALONE TO WORK ON IT. IT WAS amazingly difficult. I could remember a lot of things, but I couldn't seem to get them in the right order. It was easiest to remember what Linda said, like, "You said you had good nerves. Sure. Nothing could rattle you. Just plan and wait. No loose ends." And the part about the cigarette butts. And about being so demure it sickened her.

I kept thinking of things I had forgotten, and then making marginal notes about where they should be inserted.

It was dusk when Hill and a guard came and got me and took me down to the small room where they had first interviewed me. He read over what I had written. He had me wait there with the guard. He was gone over an hour. When he came back he had four typed copies of what I had written. He had four people with him, two young girls and two men. He didn't introduce them. He merely said, "Paul, these people are professionals. I got them down here from Sarasota. I've briefed them a little. I want you to check the voices, pick the two closest to Linda and Jeff."

One of the girls was pretty good. Neither of the men seemed close. I told Hill that and he said I didn't have to worry too much about that, just to pick the one which sounded nearest. Hill thanked the two who weren't right, and they asked if they could stay and listen. He said they could, but when all of them left, they should remember that this was a very confidential matter.

I do not know how many times they went over it. Sandwiches and coffee were brought in. The guard lost interest and kept yawning. I got over my original reticence and coached them as to how the lines were said. The girl kept trying to sound too dramatic, and the man had a tendency to speak too slowly. I could tell that some parts were surprisingly right, and others weren't so good. It seemed that they didn't sound right because I didn't have the words right. And it surprised me the way the right words came back to me when they would say the wrong ones.

Finally, I was as satisfied as I could get, even though I knew that those two didn't actually sound anything like Linda and Jeff. They had the emphasis right, and the speed and the sort of secretive sound of it, but it just wasn't right.

It was then that Hill brought in the machine. It was an ordinary dictation machine, of a kind seen in many offices. He had them do a portion of it and then he played it back. He said, "We'll have to take it further from the mike, kids. You come through too clearly. Let me erase what we've got, and then we'll try it about here. Okay?"

He made a second test, erased, and let them go all the way through it. It shocked me when he played it back. Their voices, through the imperfections of the recording equipment, had lost that individual tone quality that set them apart from Linda and Jeff. They could have been Linda and Jeff. It was uncanny. Some parts were so vividly real that my neck tingled. Other parts were not so good.

After I had heard all of it, Hill played it again, telling me to listen closely and indicate the best part, the most perfect part. It was where he said, "Yes, you really have to think about it, don't you?"

And she said, "Now don't start that. From the point of view of the law, my friend, it was our finger on the trigger, not just mine. Ours. Please, Jeff. Try to take it easy. Nothing can happen to us. We planned it too carefully. And don't fret about Paul. He hasn't got the guts of a rabbit."

He marked that portion on a paper tape that stretched across the front of the black cylinder. He thanked the people who had helped. The girl made a face and said, "All that practice, Dave, and then you make us sound as if we didn't have any voices at all."

"That's the way I want it," he said, smiling. "And if it works, kids, you'll get as much credit as I can give you."

IT WAS TEN IN THE MORNING WHEN THEY TOOK me down to a big office I had not seen before. Hill sat behind a big desk. His smile was quick and nervous. Sheriff Vernon stood by the windows, pouchy and ill-humored. The pimply girl sat off to the side with her steno pad. Mr. Shepp sat alone in critical dignity. They put me in a chair in the corner.

"What do you want him here for while this damn fool stunt goes on?" Vernon demanded.

"The psychological effect, I guess. Tell your guard to wait in the corridor. I want Cowley to look as if he had been freed."

Vernon reluctantly gave the order. Shepp said, "It behooves me to state at this point, officially and for the record, that I would not be a party to this were it not for the pleadings of my assistant. Is that quite clear? In addition I have grave doubts about the legality of this proceeding."

Hill said, "It won't take long. It's an experiment."

Vernon sniffed, turned his broad back to the room and looked out the window, disassociating himself from such nonsense. I sat uncomfortably. My moccasins had dried stiff and hard, pinching my insteps. The slacks were stiff with dried salt. I heard the distinctive click-tap, click-tap of her high heels, heard her voice on a rising, questioning inflection as she spoke to someone. A tall sallow man in uniform opened the door for her and she came in. She came three steps into the room and I watched her, saw her quick eyes flick around, pass across me. She wore a white blouse, fluffy and intricate, setting off her dark tan. She wore a brick red coarse weave skirt, a belt with a big silver Mexican buckle. She wore lizard shoes with four-inch heels, and I remembered that those shoes had cost twenty-nine dollars. She carried an oblong straw purse that looked like a doll coffin.

"Did you want to talk to me?" she asked the room at large.

"Please sit down right there, Mrs. Cowley," Hill said. She sat down in her neat way, crossed her good legs, lizard toe pointing toward the floor, dark eyebrows delicately raised in question. Hill rubbed the bowl of his pipe against the side of his nose, inspected the fresh gloss.

"Mrs. Cowley," he said, "purely as an experiment, and I might say contrary to the wishes of my superiors, I took the liberty of having recording equipment installed on the Dooley property."

Her face did not change. I watched her hands. She held the wide straw strap of the purse. She began to scuff at the strap with her pointed thumbnail. It made a faint mouse-sound in the still room. "Yes?" Eyebrows still delicately raised.

"Mr. Cowley advised that you were shrewd enough to be on guard while in either of the cottages. While you were driving to pick up Mr. Jeffries on his return, I looked over the property and decided to have the installation made in that overturned boat near the bay dock."

"I'm afraid I don't understand all this," Linda said politely. But her thumb was digging harder at the straw. She had parted some of the small strands.

"I'd like to play back some of the results," he said. He turned and fiddled with the equipment beside him, below the desk level, out of sight. The room was very quiet. I heard a girl walk down the hall, humming softly. I heard a far-off police whistle.

The equipment hissed and hummed and then the ghost voice of Jeff, crackling, disembodied, said sarcastically, "Yes, you really have to think about it, don't you?"

"Now don't start that. From the point of view of the law, my friend, it was our finger on the trigger, not just mine. Ours. Please, Jeff. Try to take it easy. Nothing can happen to us. We planned it too carefully. And don't fret about Paul. He hasn't got the guts of a rabbit."

Hill turned off the machine. Linda sat very still, her head tilted to one side, her thumbnail deep in the soft strap, the cords of her throat harsh. She looked as if she was still listening to the voice. The ovoid pad of muscle between her thumb and forefinger bulged. I saw the tension go out of her hand and saw her throat soften. I do not know what went on in her mind. I suspect she detected some flaw in diction or phrasing or emphasis. She was good. She was a shrewd animal fighting for its life. She leaned back in the chair and she laughed.

It was a good laugh and it took the life out of Dave Hill's deep-set eyes. "Really, Mr. Hill, I don't understand what this is all about. Was that supposed to be me talking to Mr. Jeffries? Isn't this a little quaint?" She looked over at Vernon. "Is this your idea of police work?"

"Not my idea, ma'am," Vernon said.

"All right, Jenneau," Hill said to the guard. "Take her to Room 12 and leave her with Mrs. Carty, and bring Jeffries in here."

She had gotten up as Hill started to speak to the man in uniform. Her color was good. When Hill said to bring Jeffries in, I saw her eyes change and I knew that in that moment she knew exactly what would happen. The area around her mouth turned gray and bloodless under her tan. Her smile as she turned toward Shepp was grotesque.

"I think we've had quite enough of this nonsense," she said. "I don't see why Mr. Jeffries should be subjected to this sort of farce."

"I agree wholeheartedly," Shepp said in his bassoon voice. "We've had enough of this embarrassing farce, Hill. I'm calling it off right now. I've never had the sightest doubt in my mind but what—"

"Hold it!" Vernon said. He stood there, looking at Linda. The eyes in his fat, sweaty, sick-looking face were shrewd. He looked at Linda for a few more seconds. He nodded, as though deciding something within himself. "Do just like Hill told you, Jenneau."

Shepp stood up. "But I insist that—"

"Sit down and shut your face!" Vernon said, never tak-

ing his eyes from Linda's face. He smiled at her. It was
not a smile I want anyone to give me. She turned violently
away and they left the room.

Hill said softly, "Thanks."

It was a long two minutes before Jeff came in. Big, rugged, hearty Jeff. Gray sports shirt with green fish on it.
Material taut over the shoulders. Spiky bushcut, and en-
gaging grin.

"Sure," he said cheerfully and sat where Hill told him to
sit. "Glad to help in any way I can."

Hill gave him exactly the same build-up he had given
Linda. I had the curious impression that, as Hill spoke,
Jeff was dwindling before my eyes, shrinking down into
himself. The recording was, of course, exactly the same as
before. The rasping ghost voices.

Jeff did not break the long silence that followed the
recording.

Hill said, in a kindly tone, "We have all of it. The entire
conversation. Would you like to hear all of it?"

Jeff did not answer. I could not see his expression. I saw
the big chest lift and fall with the slow cadence of his
breathing. I realized that he was frozen there with terror
and regret, and some animal caution told him that the only
thing he could do would be to say nothing.

"Mrs. Cowley has informed us that it was your plan
from the very beginning."

I expected several things. A heated denial. A wild at-
tempt at escape. I did not expect what he did. He put his
big hands up and held them, palms flat against his face.
He bent forward from the waist. The sobs were vocalized.
"Ah-huh, ah-huh, ah-huh—" the phrasing and emphasis
of a small child that cries, but projected grotesquely in a
stifled baritone. Small, grown-up child, lost and alone. It
made me acutely uncomfortable. I shifted uneasily. Hill
was frowning. Vernon looked at Jeffries with heavy contempt. Shepp looked astounded.

No one spoke. Jeff slowly regained control. He snuffled,
wiped his nose on the back of his hand. He sat with his

elbows on spread knees, forehead resting on his fists as though he could not bear to look at anyone.

"It wasn't . . . my plan," he said, his breath catching from time to time. Hill nodded at the girl. She began to take notes. "Some of it was mine. The live fish. And the kind of gun. It started as a joke. After we started . . . seeing each other. I'd tell her how tight Stella was with her money. She'd tell me how dull Paul was. I think she was the one who said it would be nice if—if they dropped dead. I said Paul . . . ought to murder Stella and hang for it. Joking. Just joking like that. But . . . it grew. We talked about ways it could happen. Where it should happen. We had a lot of bad ideas. Then we had this one. It's funny. Right up until . . . right up until the last second, I was . . . thinking about it like it was . . . a plan that wasn't really real. Wouldn't really happen. Then . . . she did it. She shot Stella in the head and that made it real and we . . . had to go through with it."

He looked at Hill then. He said carefully, explaining it, "Once the shot was fired, you couldn't take it back. You couldn't change anything."

"No," Hill said gently, "you couldn't change anything."

"I didn't mean to do it," Jeff said.

THERE ISN'T MUCH MORE. I DID ONE THING I'M sorry about. I had them let me in to see her. I looked through the bars at her. I had expected that she would be just the same, cold and fierce and haughty, even though they'd had her for three weeks. I wanted to call on her the way she'd called on me. I thought her eyes would flash at me and she'd make cruel hooks of her nails. But she just sat on the bunk. Her tan had faded a lot and she had put on a lot of weight. Her black hair was a mess and she didn't have any make-up on. She had turned middle-aged in three weeks, and the new weight she had put on looked doughy. She looked at me with dull eyes and the lower part of her face was slack, the way it had been when I took the gun away from her.

She looked away from me. I stood by the bars and I said, "Linda." She didn't look at me. My eyes stung. I wasn't crying for her, I guess. I was crying for the unknown girl named Linda I had once lived with.

At the trial they seemed like strangers. They didn't look at me when I testified. I went back north after the trial. I worked in my shop in the cellar all through the night before the early morning when they were executed. I washed my hands in the cellar sink and hung up the sawdusty coveralls and went up into the kitchen. I looked at the electric clock she had bought. It was pottery, shaped like a plate. It was twenty past the hour and I knew it was over. I filled a glass with water and drank it slowly, looking out at the yard. The house was empty, and the world too seemed peculiarly empty. I felt as though I should do something dramatic, decisive, final. There seemed to be some great gesture I could perform, if I could only think of what it was.

In the end, all I did was shower, shave and drive to the office. I was early. When Rufus came in he told me I could take a day or week off if I felt like it.

I told him I felt all right.

ABOUT THE AUTHOR

John D. MacDonald was graduated from Syracuse University and received an MBA from the Harvard Business School. He and his wife, Dorothy, had one son and several grandchildren. Mr. MacDonald died in December 1986.